THE DREAM GATHERER

A Green Rider novella

And other stories

KRISTEN BRITAIN

GOLLANCZ

LONDON

First published in Great Britain in 2018 by Gollancz
an imprint of the Orion Publishing Group Ltd
Carmelite House, 50 Victoria Embankment
London EC4Y 0DZ

An Hachette UK Company

1 3 5 7 9 10 8 6 4 2

A CIP catalogue record for this book is
available from the British Library.

ISBN (trade paperback) 978 1 473 22644 9
ISBN (eBook) 978 1 473 22646 3

Printed in Great Britain by Clays Ltd, Elcograf S.p.A.

MIX
Paper from
responsible sources
FSC® C104740

www.kristenbritain.com
www.gollancz.co.uk

In memory of my crazy boy,
my red Gryphon,
and Writer Dog,
whose loving companionship
during the creation of this book,
was his final act.

September 4, 2001-September 13, 2017

Step Into a Dream

I dare you.

It's not an easy thing, to let go. To hand control of your reality to someone else. To allow yourself to be changed.

For that happens, in a dream.

They aren't safe. But they shouldn't be. The best dreams take you where you didn't plan to go. Show you who you didn't expect to meet. Carve memories, as vivid as any you live by the light of day. *Change* you.

Especially when the author of a dream sculpts the land beneath your feet, curls the ocean, and scents the air you breathe. When she reveals past, present, and, yes, future. When she paints with such urgent magic.

By her craft, in her care? Dreams turn the world. They disturb. Toss waves and rock boats. Trouble what's hidden. Awake the forgotten.

Expose truths.

Oh, dreams aren't real, you claim. Fantasy . . . isn't. You think to read these words and come out the same?

I promise you won't. For these are Kristen Britain's words—her world, her dream. She will take you, show you, *carve* you with profound imagery and key events. You'll laugh and cry even as the land shifts, waves roar, and you walk a garden path. You'll be disturbed and troubled, joy-filled and hopeful, wrung dry of tears—and, most of all, you'll learn *truths* about yourself. Be changed, forever.

So, read. Enter this fantasy. Summon your courage, your inner Green Rider, and answer the ultimate call.

Dare.

Dream.

—*Julie E. Czerneda*
Canada, 2018

About a Friendship

Kristen and I go waaay back. Twenty years ago, her first book, the thoroughly delightful *Green Rider,* was published by DAW Books. We were introduced by her editor, Betsy Wollheim, because I was (a) another DAW author (we run in packs) and (b) active online—including my then SFF.NET newsgroup. Kristen was, with some trepidation, about to take the plunge. Betsy hoped I'd be her guide.

Not a problem. I read and loved *Green Rider,* and if experience has taught me anything, it's that the best authors reveal their true selves in their work—and trust me, that takes courage. Kristen's honesty, humor, warmth, and knowledge shine through everything she writes. It would have been more surprising had we not become fast friends. (Roger, my other half, is too.) I'm proud to say Kristen began several other lasting friendships via my newsgroup. Yup. Sucked her right into the fold. So many Canadians! As I've made friends through Kristen—to find myself in Bar Harbor, witness to the fabulous landscapes captured in her series. (Hi, Mel!)

Since, we've thrown fruit at one another, dodged hummingbirds on our deck (yes, they're a little bit our fault), attended conventions and DAW Dinners™, and always shared the ups, downs, and sideways that are writing, and life. Kristen appeared as a dastardly villain in one of my books, at her behest, requiring the invention of a drink called "Pink Rider."

And, in case you're curious, Roger and I continue to play our wee role in Kristen's online presence. He, her website, while I keep doing my best to get her in trouble—I mean, out in front of you. (I helped her join FB while on our deck, while dodging those little red hummers.)

We will, of course, be friends for life. I will, equally of course, continue to be impressed by her work ethic, her courage, both professional and personal, and how Kristen continues to outdo herself. If you're one of her readers, believe me when I tell you no one gives more. If you aren't, yet, join us!

It has been an honor and privilege to add my words to yours, Kristen, in this special celebration of twenty years of your magic. Thank you for such a wonderful gift.

Your friend, Julie Cz.

The Story Behind the Story
-or-
It's Been Twenty Years *Already???* UGH.

Once upon a time, a seasonal ranger decided to decline winter positions offered to her in national parks in sunny Florida so she could experience a winter in Maine at Acadia National Park. True story. And, yes, that was me. I had worked three summer seasons at Acadia (which included parts of spring and fall) and I wanted to see the mountains mantled with snow and find out what the park was like during the quiet season without millions of summer tourists crowding it. I guess I just wanted to experience the year full circle in one of my favorite places. Also, I had moved from one park to another nine times in four years and I was ready to sit still for a while. Finally, and perhaps most importantly, I would be working only part-time that winter at the park, which meant I could devote the rest of my time to writing.

I had been writing all along since I was a kid. In the fourth grade I began my first novel (which I eventually tore up), and I'd written and finished a novel as a teen. As an adult, I still wanted to write novels, but all the writing advice I was seeing at the time said that in order to break in with a publisher, one must acquire short story credits. (I will note here that such credits *are* helpful to catch the eye of an agent or editor, but, as I eventually learned, *not* necessary.) So I tried all sorts of short stories with all sorts of publications. The problem was nobody wanted the kind of stories I wrote, and it seemed few editors published the kinds of stories I was interested in (traditional and adventure fantasy). And, yes, I admit my skill was nascent at the time and probably not up to snuff. In any case, out of frustration, beginning in the fall of 1992 at Acadia, I decided to forget short stories and concentrate on my first love: novels. I had no idea what I was getting myself into.

Writing the first draft of what turned out to be *Green Rider* was fun, a bright and shiny adventure. I pulled an end table from the living room of the apartment I shared with my ranger friend Kate at park HQ and put it in my bedroom, and on it I placed my 80/88 XT Magnavox computer. Then I dragged in a straight-back dining room chair to sit on (yes, ouch). I placed the keyboard on a pillow, which went on my lap so I could type. My kitten, Batwing, sat on the pillow between me and the keyboard.

I'd start earlyish in the morning and write for up to ten hours or more a day, making up the story as I went. My "mental" outline went something like this: *Girl runs away from school, meets a dying messenger on the road and agrees to carry his important message to the king, gets into all kinds of trouble along the way, and delivers message.* It was fun coming up with what trouble I was going to throw at Karigan next and how she was going to get out of it. I think the key word here is "fun." If I hadn't been having fun, likely I would never have finished that first draft. Alternatively, if I had finished it, readers would have picked up on my disenchantment pretty quickly and set the book aside.

Long days of writing required breaks now and then, and helped the writing process along. I'd walk down to Aunt Betty Pond to watch autumn hues harden into cold, stark winter, or I'd make a mug of hot chocolate as wind pushed snowdrifts against my window. On weekends I'd read to Kate what I had written during the week. In a sense, she was my first reader (or rather, listener). (Unless you count Batwing.)

I always think back on that first winter with a great deal of fondness. The novel-writing adventure had just begun, and there was no pressure placed on me, no expectations from publishers or anyone. I was young and relatively unburdened by mortgages or other adult concerns, my life fit into the back of a Subaru wagon, and I was in love with Acadia.

I finished the first draft the following summer. The manuscript was not long, but I was really pleased by the fact I'd written an actual novel. Finishing the first draft, however, was only the first step. I revised and polished, researched publishing at the local and state libraries (the internet wasn't really a thing back then), revised and polished, participated in writing workshops to hone my skills, polished and revised, submitted the manuscript to agents and editors, and collected rejections. I continued to try to make the manuscript better with, yes, more revising and polishing.

It took four years to create a novel that would be acceptable to an agent and publisher. Key to this in the final revision was a newly published fantasy author who lived nearby and graciously agreed to do a read-through of my manuscript. His name was Terry Goodkind, and he turned out to be not just a great writer, but a great editor, too, pointing out plot flaws and bad character names, among other issues. It was also a relief to me to be able to talk to someone on our relatively rural island about fantasy.

I submitted the novel to Terry's agency. When agent Anna Ghosh phoned offering to represent me, I was so excited that night I kept sitting up in bed and saying aloud in the dark, "I've got an agent!" I am sure the cats—Batwing was now joined by an orange tabby named Percy—wondered what the heck was wrong with their food provider and servant.

Anna circulated the manuscript to houses that published science fiction and fantasy. There were a couple bites fairly quickly. On November 5, 1996, I accepted an offer from Betsy Wollheim of DAW Books, Inc., to publish *Green Rider* and an untitled, unwritten sequel (which eventually became *First Rider's Call*). DAW was a natural fit for me if all the DAW Books on my shelves crowding out other publishers was any indication. That day was also a presidential Election Day, and I remember heading down to the polls after the call and standing in line to vote, smiling ear to ear. After all the years of work, my dreams were coming true. It felt like the world had opened up and anything was now possible.

It would be two long years before *Green Rider* was released, but there were little thrills along the way, like talking to Betsy for the first time. After all, she was famous to me for publishing the likes of Tad Williams, Jennifer Roberson, Mercedes Lackey, and several other beloved fantasy and science fiction authors. A lot of our initial conversation is a fog to me now since it was so long ago and I was taking cold medication at the time, but I remember her asking, "What do you think about the cover?" I was shocked because popular wisdom held that authors should not expect to be allowed input on covers, but over time I learned that DAW does things its own way, as it is a small family company, not a major corporation, run by Betsy and copublisher Sheila Gilbert.

In answer to Betsy's question about the cover, I blurted, "Keith Parkinson!" Why would I not? He was one of the top fantasy artists, and I had seen the beautiful originals to the covers of *Wizard's First Rule* and *Stone of Tears* on the walls of Terry's house. Keith's vivid and realistic style really appealed to me, and did I mention how *beautiful* his work was? I then backtracked and asked Betsy if that was what she wanted to know. We discussed what image should go on the cover, and I said, "Someone in green riding a horse." Hey, it made sense to me, and that's what we got, but more gorgeous than I could have imagined. How lucky was I to have a Keith Parkinson cover on my first book?

Betsy also mentioned the possibility, in that initial conversation, of publishing *Green Rider* in hardcover. Hardcover! I later found out that I would be only the second DAW author in the company's history to debut in hardcover. The first was Tad Williams with *Tailchaser's Song* in 1985. A paperback edition would follow a year or more later, which was great. It was the era of the big box bookstore, and of the smaller mall bookstore. There were no e-books at this time, so shelf space in bookstores was important, meaning that two different editions at two different times meant more eyeballs on my book.

I received an early copy of the book at my office a month or two before it was due to be released. That day I was assigned to staff Acadia's Nature Center, and at lunchtime I stole away to the Tarn (small body of water beneath Dorr Mountain) to look at the book. There was my name embossed on front! I admired the cover and print and endpapers, and the luminous green foil of the title. I think I slept with it in my bed that night.

The first hardcover edition of *Green Rider* was officially released in November 1998. There was no champagne, no ticker tape parade, no celebration. In fact, the silence was deafening. (Dial-up and internet connectivity remained poor on the island.) I remember fretting and thinking it scary that other people I did not know (and did know!) might be reading my book. I hoped they would like it. That was twenty years ago and I do wonder where all the time went. Writing the sequels,

I guess, but all that came after *Green Rider* is a story for another day.

Here are some things you may or may not know about *Green Rider*:

- Karigan started out as a minor male character who was a messenger, but then *he* decided he wanted to be a *she*, and suddenly *she* was full of story potential and thus became the main character. The adage "Don't kill the messenger!" suggested to me that messengers led exciting and dangerous lives, which meant lots of story fodder. Plus horses!

- Karigan's name. There must have been figure skating on television as I began work on the manuscript, with U.S. figure skater Nancy Kerrigan doing her thing, because the name "Kerrigan" resonated with me. Hence, Karigan's name.

- Condor, Karigan's horse, was inspired by a gangly chestnut gelding named Carefree I used to ride as a kid. He was good-natured and reliable to ride, and my favorite lesson horse.

- Speaking of which, during the writing of Green Rider, part of my job at Acadia was to rove the park's historic system of carriage roads to encourage safe and courteous use by visitors walking, bicycling, and horseback riding on them, and to interpret for visitors the significance of the roads as well as Acadia in general. As I went about my duty, it was easy to envision a messenger on her trusty steed riding through the forest. Alas, my trusty steed was a mountain bike, and I doubt Karigan would have been stopping so often to remind people to keep their dogs leashed.

- In the first draft of Green Rider, just about the only point of view was Karigan's. We didn't have point of view scenes from old Mirwell or Amilton. The manuscript was much shorter and may have ended just after the Battle of the Lost Lake (hard to remember that far back). I probably added about 75,000 words' worth of story to it. I took out a lot, too, including the first twenty pages that showed Karigan at school beating up Timas and preparing to run away. It was Terry who suggested I lop it off, and he was right. It improved the beginning a great deal.

- Over that first winter of writing, I read the Anne of Green Gables books by L. M. Montgomery. In Green Rider, my creation of the Berry sisters was sort of inspired by the ambience and time period of the Anne books. In homage, when Karigan stays the night with the sisters, she sleeps in the east gable bedroom.

- Seven Chimneys, the house of the Berry sisters, was architecturally inspired by the French Romanesque Revival-style gatehouse (or, more properly, gate lodge) I was housed in during my first summer at Acadia in 1989. Across from Jordan Pond, the quaint stone-and-timber house with its leaded windows has always been a popular draw for visitors who wander over to check it out. It was a cool place to live, but I bet the sisters didn't have strangers peering through their windows all hours of the day, or cameras flashing in the windows at night.

- Acadia inspired the environment/landscape of Sacoridia. When I began writing, I did not want to set the book in a traditional European landscape (of which I knew too little) or some generic landscape. Why not an American landscape? I imagined castles in Maine and liked the notion. Sacoridia is not a literal representation of Maine, but it is Mainelike. It has also worked well for the world building. Like the economy in Maine, for instance, Sacoridia's economy is based largely on natural resources—forest products, shipbuilding, fishing, quarrying, etc. One industry that is one of the largest in Maine but not in Sacoridia is tourism. *I'd visit Sacoridia for real if I could.*

- Finally, why *Green* Rider? Well, Pink Rider didn't sound right (or look aesthetically pleasing in my mind). Green made sense since Sacoridia was densely forested, allowing messengers with their dangerous jobs to blend in better with their surroundings if hunted by bad guys. It is also true that green was part of my ranger uniform.

That long-ago day when a runaway schoolgirl agreed to carry on a dying Green Rider's message errand, it changed the course of her life, and mine, too. Twenty years later, here I am working on book seven of the Green Rider Series, still tormenting my characters. It hasn't been an easy ride, but I can't imagine anything else that I'd rather be doing. I hope you enjoy the stories that follow. They are my personal celebration of the twentieth anniversary of the publication of *Green Rider*.

May yours be a Wild Ride!

—*Kristen*

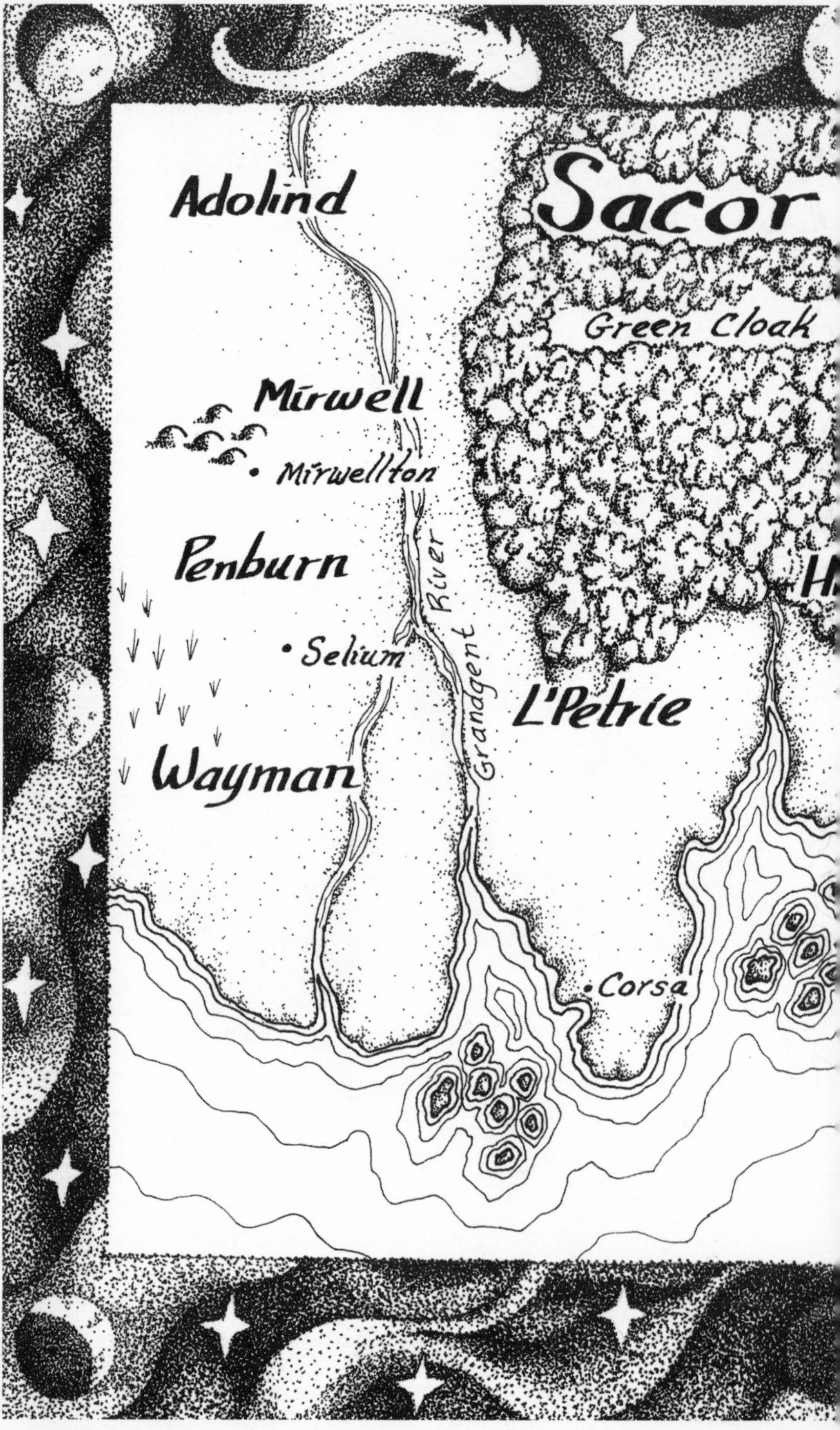

Adolind
Sacor
Green Cloak
Mirwell
Mirwellton
Penburn
River
Grandgent
Selium
L'Petrie
Wayman
Corsa

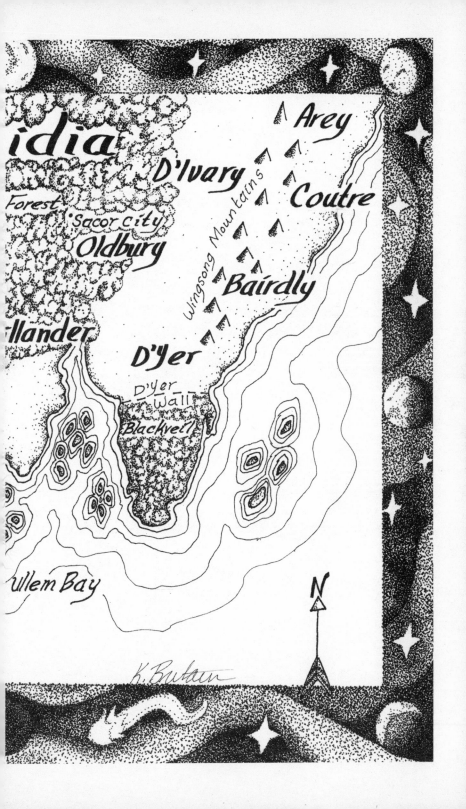

WISHWIND

From *Karigan G'ladheon and the Green Riders: A History* by Lady Estral Andovian Fiori, the Golden Guardian of Selium

Vol. 1, Appx. F "Legends of the Past"
(2) Legend of Marin the Gardener, Rider Danalong, *Wishwind*, Northern Sea Archipelago

Records about Green Rider history from more than two hundred years ago are frustratingly rare due to the time period, the general lack of respect for messengers, and purges of documents related to magic after the war. Perhaps the worst damage was committed by King Agates Sealender, who, in his hatred of his own messengers, sought to destroy anything he could about the Green Riders.

Much of what we know today has been passed down in oral tradition, though most found the Green Riders unworthy of even that form of historical acknowledgment. Some four hundred years ago, one Selium minstrel, called Wallsin the Younger, took an interest in oral history and wrote down several stories to preserve them. His manuscripts remain in Selium's archives. He saw fit to include a tale about a Green Rider named Danalong. Marin the Gardener, long a figure of Sacoridian myth, also plays a prominent role in the story.

Though set during the Long War, the story was recorded six hundred years after peace settled over the lands. Did the Marin myth originate during the Long War, or was she added in as the story was passed down from generation to generation? Or perhaps her existence in myth pre-dated even the ancient time of the Long War. What of Rider Danalong? Was he someone who really lived? How accurate is this account? Other documents support the details of a decisive battle along the Coutre coast referred to in this tale, in which Arey supplied King Jonaeus with reinforcements to repel Mornhavon the Black. But what of Danalong himself? It is unlikely we'll ever know.

Wishwind

Danalong's nostrils flared with the scents of the ocean and his own blood. He staggered inland shedding droplets of seawater on the forest floor. Step by painful step, he was guided only by the pale gleam of moonlight.

Wet and racked by chills, he gasped for breath as if drowning, but he was on dry land. It was his comrades, his people, who had drowned. The sea had lashed out and the wind had twisted around, thrusting *Windswift* onto a hidden shelf, gutting it of cargo, crew, and soldiers. The cries and shouts, horses screaming as they spilled into the waves, the crack of masts as they splintered and toppled. The roar of ocean filling Danalong's ears. Swallowing great gulps of water, swirling in the waves, drowning, drowning . . .

Then his flailing hands had fallen upon a plank of wreckage that appeared out of the darkness like a gift bestowed upon him by the gods, and on this he floated to the shore of an unknown island. The surging ocean had slammed him into barnacle-clad rocks that shredded hands, elbows, and knees. Now the cool night air stung the raw wounds.

He shoved aside tree limbs and crashed through underbrush with drunken momentum, driven inland by instinct, or some force he could not name. Abruptly the thick forest gave way and he stumbled into a moonlit clearing. A vision appeared before him of an ivory-haired woman singing of autumn apples to a fawn as its mother and a bobcat watched on.

Impossible! he thought, and the world darkened.

Danalong thrashed in the water, waves crashing over his head. The current tried to pull him back under and fill his nose and mouth. The sea took young Jaren and Avery, and Drake and the others. Drawn under one by one, their pale faces and limbs faded beneath the water's dark surface.

"No!" he cried and realized he wrestled with blankets and not the ocean. Sunshine and the scent of evergreens flowed through a window above where he lay on a coarse mattress and eased his panic. He was in a one-room croft of stone and the hearth crackled with a day fire. Dried herbs hung from the rafters above. A table laden with bread, honey, and berries occupied the center of the room. All else was obscured in contrasts of sunlight and shadow.

Might this be Coutre Harbor, he wondered, and the wreck no more than a nightmare? He listened for a time to the piping song of a thrush outside and the rustling of leaves in a breeze. No, not Coutre Harbor, he decided, which would be rank and noisy as a busy seaport always was. The wreck had been no nightmare. The *Windswift* was truly gone.

"No," he whispered. He'd been on a vital mission for King Jonaeus to gather Lord Arey's troops and lead them to the coast of Coutre, where intelligence said Mornhavon's forces planned an assault. If Mornhavon took the eastern provinces, it would cost the Sacor Clans the war, and all the years of suffering and slaughter would be for naught. Now with the ship's loss, the king would receive no reinforcements at all, for

Windswift's sister ship, *Wishwind,* carrying additional troops and supplies, had vanished in a gale days ago.

He recalled strong currents and high waves as they approached the Northern Sea Archipelago. It had been the shipmaster's plan to use the islands to conceal their approach from Mornhavon's spies despite the archipelago's dangerous tides and currents. Even more perilous in the minds of some sailors was the archipelago's reputation for the uncanny. Rife in the dark berths of ships and the taverns of every port town were tales of witches casting spells over unwary mariners and sinking ships, and of the ancient sea kings who were said to slumber in island caves until they awoke once more to dominate the lands.

The shipmaster of *Windswift* scoffed at superstition and was confident in his ability to navigate the archipelago's hazards and the night's fickle winds. His miscalculation, however, not only cost countless lives aboard ship, but possibly the war itself.

Both ships lost. No hope.

The croft's door opened, and the willowy, ivory-haired woman of Danalong's previous vision stepped inside and appraised him with granite-gray eyes.

"You should eat, child," the woman said, and she gestured at the table.

"Who are you?"

"I am Marin. Eat. It is late noon and your stomach is empty."

"I must go to the shore," he said. "We were wrecked—my ship. I must help my people." Then he added more quietly, "If any survive." He held little hope that any others had survived the violence of the sea.

"Eat," Marin told him. "If there are survivors, you are in no condition to aid them at the moment."

Danalong wrapped the blanket around himself for under-neath he wore only his own skin. His clothes dried before the fire. When he sat at the table he just stared at the food unable to actually eat. Marin broke off a piece of bread and spread it with honey and placed it in his hand.

"You must find your strength again. You are no good to anyone right now, Green Rider, least of all yourself."

He obeyed but did not taste the food. His mind was too full of the previous night's disaster and wondering about this Marin woman who seemed to know who, or at least what, he was, though his green cloak and winged horse brooch would've given that away. Still, her manner was *knowing*. He felt no threat from her, but found her penetrating gaze and silence uncomfortable.

Finally, when he finished, Marin spoke. "Your clothes are dry if you choose to wear them."

He hadn't much hope for his uniform to be in any condi-tion to wear, but discovered the tunic and trousers had been stitched and patched, and the cloak was in fine shape. Once dressed, he exhaled in relief, feeling more himself.

Marin led him outside for fresh air. The croft, cloaked by flower-specked vines, sat by a lake. It was as placid as the sea had been furious.

Marin scurried to and fro inspecting flowers and trees, chattering to them like old friends. Danalong followed slowly and stiffly, shoulders erect and hands clasped behind his back. He wondered how this Marin woman had come to live on this island the charts indicated was uninhabited, and found her obvious joy in the surrounding nature eccentric. Danalong had been born into war, had grown up in an or-phan camp, his own face mirrored in those of the other children—pinched with starvation as they were forced to

8

fletch arrows, or labor in forges and tanneries in service to the war effort. When they grew strong enough to wield the weapons they made, they were sent off to fight. Child warriors returned as grim veterans missing limbs and eyes, haunted by all they had witnessed. If they returned at all.

To Danalong, nature was important only in how it affected troop movements and strategy, how it could prove an advantage or disadvantage in a given battle. How it could sustain armies. In and of itself, he had given it little consideration, and the only flowers he ever noticed were those placed on graves.

"I heard how the ocean carried you ashore." Marin could have been speaking to the trillium blossom she cupped in her hand.

"My people . . . " Their screams echoed like a fresh wound in Danalong's mind. All he could see were bodies with familiar faces floating among the wreckage.

"It happens." Marin sighed. "Your shipmaster misjudged the wind."

Danalong clawed back a wisp of hair. "The wind turned on us."

"Don't blame the wind, child," was the gentle reply. "It is not the first time nor the last. I know that you're worried about the war now that those on the battlefront will be denied aid against the invaders. You are angry because among their leader's atrocities against your people, he burned the woodlands of your coastal home. A pity, for those were ancient and goodly trees."

They had been Danalong's only refuge as a child. "How do you know so much?"

"I hear and see things."

Sea witch, Danalong thought. She had to be. Why else

9

would she be living on this island? She must scry for her knowledge with magic. He had felt no threat from her, but now he gazed after her in suspicion as she continued along the path. Maybe she was even one of Mornhavon's sorcerers and she had actually caused the demise of both ships. He knew magic only as a weapon, and, among the Green Riders, his was the deadliest of all.

A sudden unearthly cry stopped him in his tracks. He reached in reflex for a sword that was not there, a sword he'd thrown into the ocean along with his armor so they would not drag him down into the depths.

"The loon is back!" Marin pointed to the near shore of the lake.

A loon. Of course. Danalong relaxed. Loons were rare on the mainland for war had ravaged much that had been beautiful, including the lakes.

The loon floated low in the water among reeds, then dove without so much as a splash.

"He has just returned from winter on the ocean." Marin gazed long at the lake, her eyes distant. "Ancient is the loon's kind. They knew this land long before humankind ever stepped foot upon it. Before even the Eletians. And while other creatures may pass from existence and memory, the loons remain, surviving many millennia, no matter the travails of the lands."

The loon reappeared farther down the lake and called out again, a haunting sound.

"And sometimes I think," Marin continued, "they were gifted with the voice to express the loneliness of the ages in a way we cannot."

They lingered by the lake with its plash of waves and the fresh scent of spring growth. Serenity enveloped Danalong, but then he frowned and shook himself as if from a spell. The lulling quality of the lake had distracted him from the tragedy of the *Windswift*. How could he stand here in this beautiful place when his companions had perished? And yet, he could not express his sorrow. He learned as a child that tears would never bring back his family or friends, and had since hardened himself against weeping.

I can only honor the lost and redeem myself in battle, he thought. His way was to seek vengeance, but it brought only bitter solace. And one question recurred after every battle, and now after the shipwreck: *Couldn't I have saved some of them?* His special magical ability was of no help when it came to *saving* lives.

"It may seem harsh," Marin said as if reading Danalong's thoughts, "but life is for survivors."

Danalong turned on Marin. "You would say that after all I've lost? The wreck, friends killed in the fighting? Lives lost because the invaders want our land and resources? Mornhavon tortures and enslaves the innocent."

Marin sighed heavily. A breeze rippled across the lake. Cattails tossed in its wake and poplar leaves quaked. The air cooled as dusk gathered, and a full moon rose milky white to bob above the treetops.

Danalong still faced Marin, awaiting a response, his body rigid. The wisp of hair now clung damply to his forehead. Shadows grew long before Marin answered.

"I do not lean toward the ways of those like Mornhavon. There have been many such as he through the ages of this world, but like all else, they've crumbled to dust with time. They fight for dominance as eaglets in the nest, the strongest killing its sibling. Survival." Marin clasped Danalong's hand. "Child, you are a survivor. You survived a shipwreck and the violence of the sea. Tomorrow we shall garden, and then maybe you will understand."

Gardening? When he had survivors to look for? He also needed to reach the king to warn him no aid would be arriving from Arey.

"I appreciate your help," he told Marin. "You've been very kind. But, as much as I'd like to . . . garden, I've survivors to search for. And might you have a boat? I must reach King Jonaeus. It is quite urgent."

"The young ones are always in such haste." She clucked her tongue. "Child, the healing of wounds takes time, and there is no better salve than gardening."

"But—"

"As for a boat?" She chuckled. "Now what would *I* do with a boat?"

"But I need to—"

"Hush, child. Tomorrow we garden."

A warmth seemed to radiate from Marin that soothed Danalong's fury. Yes, wounds needed healing. He exhaled a deep breath, and watched in fascination as she turned her palm upward and a star seemed to settle on it to light the way.

For all Danalong could tell, Marin possessed no garden. He'd been awakened at sunrise to help, but there was no tilling of soil or weeding. Indeed, Marin proclaimed that weeds had a place in *her* garden. Her idea of gardening, as it appeared to Danalong, was simply a walk in the woods.

"Waste of time," he muttered. "My wounds are healing and I need to go."

Marin pretended, he was fairly sure, not to hear him and

skipped ahead in a careless, girlish way. He trailed along in bemusement as she pointed out trees and flowers and named them. To a cluster of low-growing white flowers alongside the trail, she sang:

Bunchberry, bunchberry,
How very merry
Your bright orange blossom berries!

Danalong lifted a brow, still uncertain of how to accept Marin's constant changes from wise woman to she child.

"They all have names so we must call them by name," Marin said. She sniffed the air. "I think the wind is suggesting rain."

Danalong wasn't surprised when, shortly after, the sky darkened and the first drops thunked on his head. Marin danced in the rain, singing to flowers. Either she was a witch or a madwoman, or, worse, both. This was nonsense. There were such important things going on in the world and he was stuck on an island with a madwoman. Her enthusiasm, however, proved infectious. It tugged at him, at the true child within that he'd never been allowed to be. Danalong the messenger, who had seen so much battle and death, pulled off his stiff, tall boots and jumped into puddles, laughing when they splashed. Perhaps it was all right to be a little mad.

Before long, the sun emerged between clouds and a delicate silver vapor drifted up from the forest floor. Marin teased and swirled it into vague designs with her hand, but stopped short.

"Oh, Bobcat," she said, "so good to see you."

A tawny spotted bobcat appeared out of the mist to rub against Marin's leg and join their walk. Of what Danalong knew of bobcats, they tended to stay aloof of humankind.

"Bobcat came to see me the night you arrived," Marin said. "He's full of stories of hunting hare and stalking squirrel. Such a boaster! I'm sure I don't want to hear it."

Bobcat walked with them a ways, pausing only to pounce at a frog that hopped across the trail, then bounded off into the mist after something else they could not see.

"Typical feline," Marin said.

"*Who* are you?" Danalong asked.

Marin paused mid-stride. "Eh?"

"Who are you?"

"I am Marin."

"I mean, are you a witch?"

"A witch?" Marin snorted. "Am I witch because I know the ways of moon and rain? I am Marin, and I know the Earth. I learn names. Events happen as they will, child, and I have little influence."

Danalong frowned, not sure his question had been answered.

Gardening continued over several days in rain, fog, and sun. Marin led Danalong along the shore so he could search for survivors of the wreck. He did not find any, nor did he spot debris. It was disquieting. Either his former life had been a dream or he was trapped in an enchantment. He touched his Rider brooch frequently, its cold contours reassuringly real for all he loathed its power to augment his magical ability. When he tried to question Marin about the absence of wreckage, she'd shrug and caper off, and once again he'd be drawn into her songs and lessons. She taught him the names of things, and how to feel the moss between his toes and sing to trees. Daily they greeted the loon, and in the evenings they pulled starlight from the sky so they could walk and listen to the sounds of nocturnal beasts.

Gardening eased Danalong's ardor for battle, and he'd finally come to the conclusion that Marin embodied no ill intent, that she was in no way aligned with Mornhavon, for Mornhavon represented only darkness, death, and destruction. Marin, it seemed, represented only the beauty of the natural world and its cycles.

Peace so settled over him that he thought he would be content to remain on the island with Marin forever, away from the hatred and violence, no longer feeling the pain of losing those he cared about.

One evening Marin stared into the croft's cold hearth. She'd allowed the fire to die, then piled fresh kindling on the hearthstone. She made no move, however, to light it.

"I cannot boil water for my tea," she said mournfully.

"No, not without a fire," he agreed.

"Perhaps you could help."

He reached for the flint and steel on the mantel.

"No, not that way," she said.

Danalong stared hard at her. "Then, in what way would you like the fire to be started?"

She did not flinch at the coldness of his tone, nor did her gaze waver. "You could use your gift."

Anger shook Danalong's body. Even his fellow Green Riders did not ask this of him. "No."

"But you've the power to ignite the kindling, child, and the fire will boil water for my tea."

He grabbed the flint and steel and thrust them at her. "Use these. Or rub sticks together."

She did not take them. Just sat there waiting.

"Fine." He threw them on the floor and stomped outside to cool off in the night air. How could she call his curse a gift? It was a weapon he'd used often in this long, terrible war against Mornhavon's people, and not just the soldiers. He closed his eyes trying to stave off images of Arcosian villages his power had razed, of charred bodies of young and old. Although it was no worse than atrocities committed by Mornhavon against the Sacor Clans, he could not cleanse his mind of what he'd done or absolve himself of guilt.

The door of the croft creaked open, and Marin stood beside him. He looked down at her, starlight silvering her eyes.

"I am sorry I snapped at you," he said.

"I understand," she replied. "I sense the many painful experiences you've endured in your life. It is a pity that such gifts should be harnessed for war."

"It is all I have ever known. Perhaps my ancestors used their abilities otherwise, but I do not know."

"Some of your ancestors, yes; some, no. It is the way of humans, always striving one way or the other. Magic, which is also called etherea, is an element of nature like the air we breathe. It does not have a mind of its own, nor is it evil or good. Humankind uses it for many purposes the way the ore of the earth is mined and worked into swords. The ore is not inherently evil, but it is subject to the will of the one who wields it."

Danalong gazed down at his feet. "Then I am evil."

"That is not the point I am trying to make, child. What else is the ore of the earth used for?"

"Tools, pots, buckles, nails . . . I understand what you are saying, but all I see is blood on a sword."

"It takes time and healing and *trying*. Perhaps you will try to light the fire so an old woman can make a soothing cup of chamomile tea." She returned inside.

He struggled with himself, the loon's lonely cry an echo of his own pain. She had no right to ask this of him. She had no idea the horrors its use conjured. Actually, she probably did. He had told her little, but she seemed to know so much about him anyway. Fire to light kindling to boil water for tea. It sounded simple. It was how he would rather use his ability, but it had been exploited for war the moment he became a Green Rider. He shook his head and entered the croft.

Inside he found Marin sitting before the hearth, the kindling unlit.

"You are not going to let this go, are you?" he asked.

"Fire lights the night," Marin told him, "on Earth and in the heavens. Ships navigate by stars. Fire warms us and heats our food, and helps us make things. It clears the land for regrowth and regeneration, and in fact some trees will not germinate without it."

It also kills, he thought, but he did not argue. Instead he sank to his knees beside her. This was one of her lessons, he knew. He would *try*. He would try to see other than the bloody sword. He would try to light a simple fire.

He extended his hand toward the hearth. Normally his ability came with explosive rage. He could not do that here for it would burn down Marin's croft and the near woods. He swallowed hard, reined back the surge of his ability. A puff of smoke rose from his fingers.

Marin squeezed his shoulder. "You are doing fine, child."

He tried to push away the grisly scenes that played in his

mind and concentrate on making a small flame. He'd once known such fine discipline; it had been his first training, but the battlefield had required no finesse, just brute force.

Sweat slid down his face as he concentrated. He recalled Captain Ambriodhe's calming voice talking him through his exercises, to ease into it. A small candlelike flame flickered to life on the tip of his index finger. He exclaimed in triumph and then used his ability to mold it into a tiny ball like a molten marble, and tossed it onto the kindling. He sat back on his heels and watched as the wood began to burn.

"Well done," Marin said. "See how the flame merrily dances on the kindling? It consumes the wood, yes, but it will help me make tea."

Danalong wiped the sweat off his face, relieved, for once, that the use of his ability hadn't killed anyone.

The next morning, Danalong awoke to find himself alone in the croft. The table was set for breakfast as usual, but it was the first time Marin had left without him. He dressed and hurried outside.

She wasn't by the lake. He saw only the loon that barely rippled the water as it glided along, the white patches of its plumage brilliant against the dark, silken surface of the lake. Danalong followed the trails they ordinarily walked, but still there was no sign of Marin. The wind picked up and whispered through tree boughs. He wondered if they were in for a storm, but the sky was clear.

The wind grew so strong that it forced him to stumble down a path he hadn't yet walked. He tried to steer back toward the croft, but the wind blew him off course.

"All right!" he shouted. "I'll follow the trail." He didn't know to whom he spoke or why, but the wind calmed considerably at his words.

The trail was rugged with rocks and twisting roots and climbed steadily to a headland that jutted out into the sea and ended at a precipitous cliff, and here the trees and shrubs grew squat to the ground as though to steel themselves against the battering of the wind and weather. The waves were loud as they dashed against the shore far below. Marin stood at the edge of the cliff, laughing in the wind.

"Why do you laugh?" Danalong asked.

Marin's ivory hair streamed behind her and her arms were outstretched as if to embrace the world. "I laugh because the sea is strong, but has no muscle. I laugh because it pushes and pulls on the shoreline, and possesses the strength to sculpt something as ancient and unyielding as granite."

The wind changed direction. Gulls cried as their flight shifted with the air currents.

"The wind," Marin said, "moves this world as no human can."

A cormorant perched on a rocky ledge below with wings spread to dry.

Marin laughed with childlike delight. "It is the purest magic of all, this alchemy of sea and wind and earth, and, of course, fire and etherea. People may use it in an ill manner, but in the end, the people will fade away, nary a memory, and the Earth shall endure without a care."

It was, Danalong thought, an oddly comforting outlook that the world would outlast any ruin wrought by human hands.

"Come," Marin said, and she led him back down the trail to garden.

When they reached the lakeshore, the loon was silent. They could not spot it as usual.

"Something has changed," Marin said. "Perhaps autumn has called our friend away to the sea."

But it wasn't autumn, and trepidation filled Danalong's heart.

They gardened. Afternoon clouds brought rain. Mist smoked from the forest floor and Bobcat appeared with prey clenched in his jaw. The loon's head trailed along the forest floor, blood seeping into its white breast. Its wings flopped lifelessly, the perfect spotted pattern of its plumage soiled and in disarray.

Danalong fell to his knees, digging his fingers deep into earth and moss. Tears washed down his cheeks. "How could he?" How could Danalong weep for a bird when he had never shed a tear for friends he'd seen struck down in battle or drowned in a shipwreck?

Startled by Danalong's outburst, Bobcat shied into the forest with his prey.

Marin's eyes were watery, but she did not cry. She knelt beside Danalong and folded him into her arms as if he were no more than a boy. She smelled of loam and sweet fern and the salt air. "It is hard, child, the way of the world. We will mourn for our friend, the loon, but before long someone new will inhabit the lake and life will go on. Yes, I know it feels as if Bobcat betrayed you, but he thinks of survival and food, not betrayal."

"Why couldn't you stop him?"

"Stop him? It is like telling the wind not to blow. I have no influence, child, just as you had no influence when your ship crashed into the sea shelf. If it had not been the loon, it would have been some other creature. It does not mean, however, we cannot express grief for our friend's passing."

"It is so cruel."

"Cruel?" Marin seemed to ponder. "It is nature. Nature is not cruel, nor is it kind. It just is."

Danalong sniffed and rubbed his eyes. Marin was right. All the days of gardening had taught him about give and take, about balance and survival.

When finally they rose to leave, a pair of wood ducks alighted onto the lake's surface.

"New neighbors and very colorful," Marin said. "There's a power in nature, you know."

Danalong thought of how rain bogged down soldiers, fire burned forests, and windstorms wrecked ships.

"You're thinking of the negative, child. Remember your lessons and think of the other side, and head for the ocean to see what the wind may bring."

Danalong turned away from Marin and gasped. His sword leaned against an oak tree.

"How did you . . . ? How did you retrieve my sword from the ocean?" he asked. When no one answered, he looked over his shoulder. Marin was gone.

"What? Marin?" He turned round and round, but there was no sign of her. Even the path they'd walked seemed to have disappeared.

Why did she leave him? Was this some new lesson? She would reappear if she wished, but he'd a growing suspicion he'd never see her again, and he stood there with a heavy heart until his gaze fell once more upon his sword. An oak staff was propped beside it. Oak was the grandmother tree of peace. He hefted the staff, liking the weight of it. The sword, in contrast, felt strange in the hand it had calloused.

Dusk followed Danalong as he bushwhacked through forest undergrowth. He let instinct guide him. The moon brightened

21

the forest as it had the night of the wreck. Soon he heard the chuckle of the ocean and the tree line gave way to a cove with a beach of rounded stones. Waves sparked wildly with moonlight. His sea-soaked uniform chilled him.

"What?" But before he could marvel over his uniform, movement on the beach caught his attention.

"Rider Danalong—is that you?" someone called.

Some of his comrades from the *Windswift* lived! But how? The *Windswift* lay gashed and broken on the sea shelf beyond the cove. He leaned on the oak staff that now appeared no more than a common branch, and pushed hair away from his eyes. He wept once more, but this time in gladness.

"Rider!" It was Jaren, the young seaman, who led a few of the others toward him. "We feared you drowned. Many have." His face grew troubled. "We've got injured on the beach shivering with the cold."

Danalong hurried to where they huddled together for warmth. Someone had collected driftwood for a fire, but it had not been lit.

"We've no flint among us," Jaren explained.

Danalong licked his lips. The injured could perish from exposure if they didn't warm up. He did not hesitate. He squatted before the wood and extended his hand. Flame grew to life over his palm and he sensed sailors and soldiers startle around him. Some knew what he could do and perhaps expected the volley of an explosive fireball to emerge from his hand, but he simply gave the flame to the driftwood and then pulled it back. As the fire grew, many drew closer to it to receive the heat. Gold-orange light flickered across grateful faces.

Jaren's face, however, was turned toward the ocean.

"What do you see?" Danalong asked.

"It is a ghost ship or I've gone mad."

Danalong squinted, unable to believe his eyes, but there a ship sailed from a fog bank looking very much a ghost ship with the unearthly glow of the moon upon it. It possessed the same gallant lines as *Windswift*. When signal lights blinked from aloft, he clapped Jaren on the back. "That is no ghost ship, it's *Wishwind*. She survived the gale."

The survivors of the wreck shouted a hurrah. A rush of wind swept their voices away, as if to another time. Danalong glanced back at the woods. Had he been inland at all? Had Marin been real? He guessed that if he searched for the croft by the lake, he would never find it.

At the forest's edge, feline eyes flashed in the moonlight.

The next morning, the first mate of *Wishwind* told Danalong how the fire on the beach had caught their attention and that if it hadn't been lit, they'd have just sailed on, never knowing the survivors awaited rescue.

As crew from the *Wishwind* rowed Danalong past the hulk of the *Windswift,* he observed that seabirds had already discovered nooks above the water in which to roost. He knew that in time barnacles would spread along its side. Fish and other creatures of the sea would find homes and protection in the ship's submerged regions, and, eventually, as the years wore on, the ocean and the weather would batter it relentlessly, causing its proud lines to rot and crumble and collapse. Ocean currents would scatter its remains on the ocean floor, and the *Windswift* would slip from human memory.

"Give and take," he murmured.

"What's that?" one of the sailors asked.

Danalong chuckled and thought he could hear another's joyous laughter on the wind. Gardening had indeed healed his wounds, and now he would help bring peace to his troubled land, and when his bones crumbled to dust, other children would be born who would try to reshape the world.

LINKED, ON THE LAKE OF SOULS

From *Karigan G'ladheon and the Green Riders: A History* by Lady Estral Andovian Fiori, the Golden Guardian of Selium

Vol. 6 Appx. R "Author Notes and Reminisces"
(10) Fictional story, told to Karigan preceding the Battle of the Lone Forest

It was following the wounding of Karigan at the hands of Second Empire's torturer, Nyssa Starling, that Karigan requested me to tell her a story to keep her mind off her pain. A made-up story, she said. I must admit I was shaken at the time by the harshness of our captivity and in fear for my friend's well-being, so it was not easy to turn my mind to the creation of stories. However, if it took making up a story to aid her, then that was what I would do. I would have done anything for her.

Knowing that Karigan, as she grew up, had loved the Journeys of Gilan Wylloland, a trove of colorful adventure tales, I dove in and told her a story—inventing it as I went along—about two bickering friends whose situation grows more dire by the moment. To save themselves they must learn to cooperate and have the utmost trust in one another. In the end, their predicament serves to deepen their friendship. I only realized some time after the fact that I had told a story about friendship to my best friend when we ourselves were in such terrible danger, but so there it is.

29

I have included this story, "Linked, on the Lake of Souls," in these appendices for the edification of those who have heard me refer to it in passing and wanted to know the whole of it.

Linked, on the Lake of Souls

Far in the northern reaches of Anglas Herad, an eagle perched high in a towering pine watched as a boat drifted on the lake below. He had seen plenty of boats before on other lakes where the humans engaged in fishing, an activity to which he could relate.

Never before, however, had he seen a boat on *this* lake, a lake even waterfowl had the wits to shun. The eagle cocked his head and blinked his golden eyes, his curiosity piqued.

The pair, he decided, were unlike the fishers he was accustomed to seeing. They dropped no netting over the side of the boat, and carried no bait. Nor did they dip paddles into the lake to propel themselves along, for they had none.

Curiouser and curiouser, the eagle thought.

The gleam of metal caught his eye and he dropped down a few branches to get a better look. One of the females was clad in a shirt of metal, but that was not all. They sat in the bottom of the boat, bound back-to-back by heavy chains, while individual sets of manacles clasped their ankles and wrists.

If all of this was not odd enough, one of the boat's occupants appeared intent on capsizing it, which would surely bring about undesired results for both.

The eagle ruffled his feathers and preened. He despaired

of humankind ever using the intelligence it was gifted with at birth. The antics of the two in the boat only seemed to confirm his low opinion of the species.

Then one of the humans cried out. The eagle paused his preening and refocused his eyes on the boat. The cry had been a warning tinged with panic.

"*Myrene!*"

The boat lurched as the warrior shifted to peer over its side. Of course, any move Myrene made, Tiphane was forced to make as well.

"What? I just want to see how deep the water is."

"Trust me," Tiphane said, "it is quite deep. Deep and icy cold."

Myrene grunted, unconvinced.

Had they not been chained together back-to-back in the bottom of the boat, Tiphane would have seen Myrene's scowl. But Tiphane did not need to see it to know it was there, for the two had been working together for nearly three years now and had grown to know one another well. Too well, it sometimes seemed.

Myrene leaned even farther over the boat's edge, hauling her chain-bound partner with her. The boat listed at an alarming angle.

"You'll capsize us!" Tiphane cried.

"I just want to find out if I can see the bottom."

"You'll see it when we overturn and that lovely mail shirt you're so fond of, along with these chains, drag us under."

Their boat, a tiny, unstable coracle, floated on silken-calm water that reflected the bright autumnal colors cloaking the mountains that ringed the lake. The lake was vast and, as Tiphane said, icy cold, for it had once been a part of the great ice sheet that still lingered in the wastes beyond the mountains. And there was more waiting in the lake's depths than Myrene could ever imagine.

"I don't intend to sink us," Myrene said. "If we aren't deep, maybe we can—"

When the coracle heeled enough for the frigid water to leak over its rim, Tiphane said, "Believe me, you don't want to see what's in the lake. There are—"

Myrene uttered a sudden, strangled cry and jerked away from the edge with such force that the flat bottom of the coracle slapped the surface of the lake. She slumped against Tiphane, her breathing ragged.

Tiphane was rather rattled herself from being wrenched around by her larger and stronger companion, and by a nightmarish vision that had flashed through her mind of the coracle capsizing and the two of them sinking inexorably downward into the lake's depths where phantom arms were outstretched to receive them . . . Perspiration glided down her temple.

"Damnation, Tiph," Myrene whispered, when finally she caught hold of herself. "Why didn't you tell me?"

Tiphane could feel Myrene trembling against her back. "I was about to tell you. I was going to tell you there is a reason it's called Lake of Souls."

The lake was crystal clear though, in the very middle where it was said to be hundreds of feet deep, the sun penetrated only so far before it gave way to the dark. Even there, however, *they* could be seen; pale hair swirling around bloodless, cadaverous faces; dark eyes staring up, mouths gaping, arms of white flesh always reaching, reaching to haul the unwary into the depths with them. There were thousands of them.

"What are they?" Myrene asked.

"No one knows exactly," Tiphane said. "Perhaps they lived here before the ice. Perhaps they are lost souls seeking the company of the living. I do not know."

Myrene, not one to spook easily, shivered. She had seen more than her share of carnage on battlefields, Tiphane knew, but what this deceptively beautiful lake concealed beneath its sun-dappled surface was another thing entirely.

A silence fell between them as the coracle, really nothing more than an oversized basket of woven willow boughs with a hide stretched over it, bobbed down the middle of the lake, tracking southward with the current.

"Are you sure you can't get the manacles off?" Myrene asked.

"I'm no lockpick," Tiphane said. "I'm a weaver of light and wind and rain, and my power cannot touch worked iron. Besides, you heard what Sedir said, and you've the runny nose to prove it."

"You've no idea how I long to wipe it." Myrene rattled her chains in frustration.

Their captor, the wizard Veidan Sedir of the Drakdorn Order, cursed be his name, had gone to great extremes to ensure their torment. The coracle was held together not with the ancient boatbuilding craft of fishermen who netted salmon on the rivers, but with magic. The moment Tiphane attempted to touch her own gifts, even for the slightest of breezes to skim them to shore, the coracle would unravel and they would sink into the waiting arms of the souls beneath the water. A cold finger of fear slithered down her spine.

They knew Sedir had not lied about the nature of the

magic that held the coracle together, for Myrene reacted to the casting of magical spells with sneezing fits. Her nose had started running the moment they were forced into the little boat.

It was a rather odd affliction Myrene suffered from, considering her constant companion, Tiphane, was a priestess who used magic as a matter of course. But it was also useful in its own way, warning them when magic other than Tiphane's was afoot. Or, it could be a liability, as in this instance, for Myrene's sneeze had given them away to Sedir as they spied upon him in his hideout.

"We're drifting to the south end," Myrene said. "I wonder what awaits us there."

"A waterfall."

"A . . . " Myrene was clearly too stunned to go on.

"It's the outlet of the lake. It drops into a gorge. That's the current pulling us along."

"How deep is this gorge?"

"Pretty deep," Tiphane replied. "You know the Great Windslo Tower?"

"Yes . . . "

"This gorge is deeper than that tower is tall." The tower was the tallest ever built, hundreds of feet high.

Myrene groaned. "That's just fine and good, isn't it. If we aren't grabbed by ghoulish hands and drowned, we'll go over the waterfall and be broken to bits at the bottom."

Myrene was not known for her subtlety, and Tiphane knew her comrade blamed her for their current predicament. It was Tiphane who had insisted they follow the trail of deaths made by Veidan Sedir, leading to his hideout in the mountains.

Sedir and his adherents practiced magic that went against

the laws of nature and Givean Herself. He was no favorite of Myrene's either, but she had preferred the option of lying low in the valley until winter forced Sedir from the mountains. It was safer, she argued, than tracking him into his own territory.

And here we are, Tiphane thought, *because I couldn't wait.* She supposed Myrene had the right of it, but she just couldn't have lived with herself if she'd allowed Sedir to run amok among the innocents who sheltered in tiny villages in the shadow of the mountains.

"We can't let Sedir wander the countryside doing blood magic at his leisure," Tiphane murmured more to herself than to her partner. "It goes against all our precepts."

"*Your* precepts. You're the Givean priestess."

"And you are my sworn Shield. Therefore you must uphold the same principles as I."

Myrene grumbled something unintelligible and sneezed, sending rings rippling outward from their coracle. Had they not been bound in chains, and had they not been floating on the Lake of Souls, it might have been an enjoyable excursion, for the scenery was breathtaking and the air, with the bite of oncoming winter in it, was exhilarating. An eagle soared through the clear sky above and screeched. Tiphane ached for its freedom.

Myrene abruptly straightened, rocking the boat.

"Can't you sit still?" Tiphane asked. Myrene tended to be all action and little thought, and it grated on more than her nerves, especially considering they were currently attached.

"I thought I saw something moving along the shore."

Tiphane craned her neck and scanned the shoreline. It was jumbled with talus from some long-ago rockslide and thick with low-growing shrubbery. Some spindly evergreens grew up between the rocks.

"I don't see anything."

"By the big boulder."

Tiphane rolled her eyes. There were hundreds of huge rocks, some the size of a shepherd's cot. "*Which* big boulder?"

"The one . . . The one . . . Damnation. I've lost it now."

Tiphane sighed in irritation, and as they drifted, she thought about how many tight spots she and Myrene had gotten themselves into over the years, ever since her mentor Radmiran had brought them together. They'd met the night she had taken the Oath of Givean, which had occurred after ten years of study and prayer. She had relinquished her family, friends, and all worldly goods to serve Givean.

The world was a dangerous place, and every priestess who chose the path of wanderer was paired with a protector. When Tiphane was in her last year of study, Myrene, a warrior who had been sold by her family to a mercenary company at a tender age, had been found among the dead after a terrible battle. Broken, bloody, and unconscious, she had been mistaken for a corpse until one of the gravediggers noticed her shallow breathing. She was brought to the Order for healing, a healing that almost failed because of her odd response to the use of magic. The priestesses had to depend mostly on conventional methods to save her.

While Myrene healed, she learned much about the good works of Givean. That, coupled with her brush with death, moved something deep within her mercenary spirit, and she changed her course in life to help others as she herself had been helped. By swearing to protect Tiphane, she swore herself to Givean.

It was understandable their tempers flared from time to time. Myrene, a woman of action, was helpless in her fetters. There was no constructive way to direct her rage, no way to lift a sword and cut down the bastard who had put them in this position, the same bastard who left the broken and shriveled bodies of people—men, women, children, the young and old alike—in his wake to foster his own powers and pay homage to Drakdorn, the god of unraveling and chaos.

Tiphane was likewise fettered, unable to touch her own magic for fear of drowning them. Of course, sooner or later, the water would take them, either in the clear, cold depths of the lake, or in the churning, whirling water pounding at the base of the waterfall.

"There it is again," Myrene said, chains clinking as she leaned forward. Water sloshed about the coracle at her sudden movement.

Tiphane scanned the distant shore, and this time she, too, saw something—someone—moving about the gigantic boulders.

"No doubt it's Sedir coming to watch us die," she muttered. "It is his kind of entertainment, us becoming one of his sacrifices."

"I would like to sacrifice *him*," Myrene said.

"You do have truly violent urges, don't you?"

"Yes," Myrene said, her voice filled with conviction.

Tiphane kept her eyes to the shore, watching for more movement. "That is not a very Givean attitude. Perhaps you should meditate on it, for Givean is the force of life, not death." Which was what made Sedir's depredations all the more loathsome to her and her Order.

Myrene snorted. "Since when has meditation saved you from bandits wielding clubs and swords on the road, hmmm? I don't think meditation is going to unlock these manacles either." She rattled the chains for emphasis.

"It has occurred to me that violent urges are not helping—"

"Look," Myrene said, cutting her off. "There are three of them."

Tiphane saw them then, a flash of bright white, which could only be Sedir's robes, followed by two darker figures, one of which seemed to be struggling.

"One of the others must be Cha'korth," Myrene said. Cha'korth was her own counterpart—Sedir's Shield.

"How much would you wager the third is another sacrifice?" Tiphane said. "It would be a good day for Sedir, you know, tormenting us by holding the sacrifice in front of us, before we die ourselves. He wants us to feel as helpless as possible."

As if to affirm their suspicions, Veidan Sedir called to them, his voice carrying easily across the water.

"Greetings, ladies! Such a lovely afternoon for boating, is it not? I thought, perhaps, I might offer you a diversion from your own forthcoming deaths."

There was a scuffling along the shore and the flash of a blade, and a scream that resounded off the mountains. When it faded, Sedir continued, "A first offering of blood to give Drakdorn a taste of what is to follow."

Myrene snarled.

"The victim looks small to me," Tiphane said, narrowing her eyes against the glare of the sun on the water. "A young boy." The boy was putting up quite a fight despite whatever injury Cha'korth had inflicted upon him. "I can't simply sit here while they commit blood magic right in front of me, and we drift to our deaths."

"Have you a plan?"

"No," Tiphane admitted. "You?"

"Maybe, and maybe not." Myrene fell into a long spell of

silence before she spoke again. "We are drifting in a current that is taking us to the waterfall, correct?"

"Correct."

"What if we got out of the current, or at least tried to get out of the direct path of the waterfall?"

Tiphane watched as Sedir, his Shield, and his victim picked their way toward the lake's outlet. Preventing their own dive over its edge would solve one problem.

"What do you propose we do?" Tiphane asked.

"If we seesaw the coracle—"

"We'll swamp it."

"Not if we're careful."

"All right," Tiphane said, "and what happens if we make it to shore?"

"You're the one with the magic."

"Hmm. I was afraid you'd say that."

She sighed, noting that their current moved more swiftly now. Sedir paused by the lip of the waterfall, looking over the area as if to decide which rock would best serve as a sacrificial altar. Myrene's idea, she decided, was better than doing nothing and helplessly awaiting their fate.

"Let's try it," she said.

Myrene and Tiphane started rocking back and forth, slowly building up momentum. Tiphane sweated with the effort, and Myrene's mail shirt abraded her back. They banged heads more than once, but they kept at it. They succeeded in splashing a lot of water about, and very nearly did swamp the boat. They gave up after that, realizing their course remained unchanged.

Tiphane grimaced as cold water soaked into the seat of her trousers.

Sedir's laughter bounced off the mountains. "Good try, ladies."

It appeared he had found his altar—a big, flat rock. Cha'korth was securing the victim to it, and Sedir was unrolling the cloth in which he stored his ritual knives. He glanced up at them, and now Tiphane could clearly see his sharp features as they drew closer.

"My robes shall be dyed in blood before I'm done," he yelled to them. Then he set about laying out his knives. Different knives for different parts of the body.

The bile roiled in Tiphane's throat. She growled in memory of the lives of the innocents Cha'korth and Sedir had cut short, and at the cruel wound the Shield had given Myrene that almost took her life a year ago.

"We need to try something else," Myrene said.

Tiphane envied Myrene her seemingly boundless determination. Maybe it was all those years she served in the mercenary company, where there was no choice but to fight or die. Tiphane, in contrast, knew they were doomed, doomed to ride over the edge of the waterfall only to be dashed on the rocks below.

Then the boat jolted and lurched without warning, and Tiphane jammed into Myrene's back with a cry, her end of the coracle rising skyward.

"What . . . ?" A hundred impolite words rushed through her mind, but she couldn't sputter a one for the fear that enveloped her.

"I'm using my feet," Myrene explained matter-of-factly. "Don't move or we'll both end up in the water." There was a loud splash, and Tiphane pictured Myrene's feet, ankle, manacles and all, plunging into the lake. She whimpered, feeling certain the boat would flip over.

There was a lot of splashing as Myrene kicked, her efforts to move the boat far more effective than their previous attempt.

"Ick!" Myrene cried. "My feet! Help me get in—they're grabbing my feet!"

Tiphane didn't need to ask *who* was doing the grabbing. She knew. They scooched and wriggled until Myrene's feet were safely in the boat.

"You did it," Tiphane said, both amazed and grateful they weren't on the lake's bottom.

Thanks to Myrene's efforts, the little coracle slipped away from the main current and spun into the eddies along the edge. By now they could hear the roar of the waterfall, but the lake had grown considerably shallower. Just yards away, grasses and boulders poked up through the lake's glassy surface.

A glimpse toward shore revealed Sedir blessing his knives one by one, now focused on his ritual. Cha'korth stood over the victim with his arms folded, his ugly, scarred face even more contorted with a grin as he watched them.

The coracle bumped into a rock, impeding further progress.

"What now?" Tiphane asked. "Water's still over our heads."

"Do some magic."

"Do—Are you mad? The boat will—"

The wizard was immersed in inscribing fire runes into the air, and a glassy cloak of magic shimmered about him. He closed his eyes, falling into a deep magic weaver's trance.

"I can't," Tiphane said. "He's wrapped in a cloak and it will deflect anything I do."

"Then inflict something on Cha'korth, and hurry."

Cha'korth's amusement at their plight had changed to suspicion, and now he drew his sword.

"Hurry," Myrene said, "do something to him. Hurt him if you can."

42

"I can't use Givean magic to hurt someone," Tiphane said. Doing so, even to Cha'korth, would pervert all she believed in.

"Well, do something—anything." Myrene's voice was pitched a note higher with urgency.

Cha'korth stalked to the water's edge. He glared menacingly at them.

Tiphane searched her scattered thoughts for an idea. A rainstorm would just drench everyone, and it would take too much energy besides. She could focus the sun on him, but he'd simply walk away with an impressive tan. No, it had to be something else, and she thought of the more spiritual side of her Order, and the words she and Myrene had exchanged about meditation.

She closed her eyes and blocked out the sound of Sedir chanting his blasphemous incantations to Drakdorn. She did not think about the glinting blade he held aloft as he stood enraptured by the dark ecstasy of his magic. Tiphane drifted deeper into her trance, feeling her own sense of joy as she sought her gift.

She delved into the deepest part of herself, to the wellspring of her spirit. It was a secluded place—deep and mysterious and tranquil. She felt no shackles about her, nor did she even feel Myrene against her back, at least not in a physical sense. Instead she found her partner's energy and life within her, like a bright burning flame. This was the link that had been forged between them when they were brought together before Givean, the night she had taken her oath.

Myrene is a part of me, she thought, *as I am a part of her.*

From this peaceful place, she wove together positive strands of fire, life, energy, balance, and love until they formed a net, which she could see only in her mind's eye, shimmering and glowing. She mentally "tossed" it at Cha'korth.

Tiphane opened her eyes. It had all taken mere seconds. Cha'korth stood stock-still, his mouth gaping, his eyes wide. His sword slipped from his hand and clattered to the ground. A burnished golden glow shone about him, and one could almost hear the harmonious flourish of harp strings . . .

And even as the glow surrounded him, Myrene sneezed lustily. "Damnation, Tiph, you cast a spell of ecstasy on him?"

Tiphane had no time to reply for the coracle disintegrated beneath them and they plunged into the freezing lake. She was unprepared and inhaled lungfuls of water. She fought to break the water's surface, but they kept sinking. Myrene struggled, too, twisting, writhing, jerking, sinking.

The water-pale faces of the lake's souls turned up to them. As they sank into a tangle of soft, pale limbs, dead fingers groped at them. A scream welled up within Tiphane that emerged as a cloud of bubbles. She was drowning, suffocating, and the souls of the lake would have them. She kicked their hands away.

Their feet met the lake bottom and they came face-to-face with the horrors. Tiphane closed her eyes and turned her face away. She felt Myrene gather herself, then launch them upward. They broke the surface sputtering and coughing, only to sink again.

When they touched bottom this time, Myrene lunged upward at an angle toward the shallows. When Tiphane realized what Myrene intended, she added her ebbing strength to her comrade's. Sink, push off, and sink again, all the while fighting the grasp of the lake's souls. Soon they no longer submerged after each lunge, and stood in water only up to their waists.

Tiphane, miserable and weak, coughed up what seemed to her to be half the lake.

"Next time you tell me to trust you," she croaked, wheezing and shivering, "remind me not to." A pale hand grabbed at her ankle. She stomped on it, almost retching again at how squishy it felt beneath her foot.

Myrene did not hear her comment. "Look," she said, "I think Sedir is starting to come out of his trance."

Tiphane's back was to the shore. "I can't see."

Myrene twisted around, almost knocking Tiphane off her feet.

"Myrene!"

"Hush, now look."

Sedir was murmuring more incantations, but his eyes were losing their glazed appearance. His magical cloak shimmered about him, and he kissed the sacrificial knife. The boy bound to the rock beneath him sobbed in fear.

"We've got to keep going," Myrene said, sniffling. "We can't let him kill that boy."

"I'm afraid I won't be much help." The use of magic exhausted Tiphane, as if she had used up much of her life force. Being half-drowned did *not* help.

"You did your part with Cha'korth," Myrene said. "Now let me do mine."

Before Tiphane could utter a single word, Myrene used their chains for leverage and hoisted her onto her back. She then waded through the shallows in a crouched position, Tiphane's legs dangling over her buttocks.

Tiphane craned her neck, but could see little beyond the sky, treetops, and mountain summits. She knew Myrene was strong, but . . .

"What are you going to do?" she asked.

"Don't know," Myrene grunted. "Sedir's 'bout out of his trance now."

Myrene's ankle chains clattered across rock as she staggered onto shore. Tiphane twisted her head, pressing her cheek against the back of Myrene's head so she could see better. They passed Cha'korth, who still stood enveloped in the spell of ecstasy, drool sliding down his chin. She brimmed with pride at a job well done.

"What's happening here?" It was Sedir, apparently fully out of his trance and much surprised by the turn of events. "You're ruining the ritual. Cha'korth! Cha'korth, to me!"

"Myrene," Tiphane said, "you've got to strike now while Sedir's between energies. If you wait, it'll be only moments before he regains his strength enough to use his power against us."

"Hold on," Myrene said, gasping.

Tiphane gritted her teeth as Myrene's lopsided gait increased in speed. "Do I have a choice?" She prayed to Givean that Myrene wouldn't trip over her chains.

"Stick your feet out. He's coming at us with a knife."

"Wha—?"

"Do it!"

Tiphane obeyed and straightened out her legs. The warrior half-loped at the best pace she could manage, chains ringing, Tiphane bouncing. The priestess thought her teeth might rattle out of her head. The next thing she knew, she was spinning, her surroundings a blur of granite, evergreen, and sky. She glimpsed Sedir briefly, his expression frozen in astonishment before her feet connected with his wrist and sent the sacrificial knife flying out of his hand in a glittering arc.

They stopped abruptly, but it seemed the world spun for a breathless, dizzying moment. Myrene panted raggedly.

"Uh oh," she said.

"What? What?" Tiphane twisted her head this way and that, but she still couldn't see what was going on.

"He looks unhappy."

"Unhappy? How unhappy?"

"*Very* unhappy. He's holding his hands out, and there is a bluish, grayish glow floating above them."

"Put me down," Tiphane said. "I need to see what he's doing."

Myrene straightened, and Tiphane slid down the accursed mail shirt. When her feet met the ground, her legs were wobbly, but they didn't fail. The two shuffled around so she could see Sedir.

Indeed, Sedir was recovering rapidly, and the spell he was weaving had a sickly cast to it. Myrene sneezed violently.

"Now what?" she asked.

Tiphane thought hard. She could not attack him directly—it would go against her beliefs, and she couldn't get around his protective cloak anyway. Not that she had much energy left for spell weaving, but there was a little reservoir perhaps, and she had Myrene oozing with all her violent urges.

Sedir's incantations reached a crescendo as the cloud of blue-gray vapor enlarged.

"Myrene," Tiphane said, "it's your turn to trust me."

"I always have," her partner said in a quiet voice. "Always."

Tiphane was touched by this admission, and wished she had not seemed to doubt Myrene in return, for she depended on her brave partner—no, not just partner, but *friend*—a great deal more than she liked to admit.

"We need to get closer to Sedir."

Without comment, they shuffled within feet of the vengeful wizard. He was so involved in his spell that he could do little to stop them. It was such times as this that a magic weaver was most vulnerable and depended on his Shield for protection. Sedir's Shield still stood on the lakeshore drooling.

"I want you to face him," Tiphane said.

Myrene's shoulders tightened, but she faced Sedir without argument. She was, after all, the Shield, and putting Tiphane's life before hers was a matter of course, and of honor. Still, it humbled Tiphane.

"Now what?" Myrene asked, her voice catching on a sneeze.

"I'm going to make a little spell. I think I have the necessary energy."

"Do it quickly then!" Myrene replied.

Tiphane was already deep within herself, shaping a globe of blue fire, calling up a gust of wind, or at the very least, a slight breeze. She molded it into the globe. Then she found that spark of light and energy belonging to Myrene, and touched it with the globe.

Myrene sneezed so explosively the two of them toppled over onto the stony ground. The gust of wind, born of Tiphane's magic and channeled through Myrene's sneeze, blew Sedir's cloudy spell back into his face. He screamed, clawing at his eyes. Red, oozing boils spread instantaneously across his flesh. He whimpered and ran knee-deep into the lake, splashing water onto his face.

Myrene clucked. "Not a good move. You would think he'd know better."

Half-wedged beneath Myrene, Tiphane wiggled around so that she might see better. Sedir paused in his splashing, looked into the water, and screamed again. Something jerked on his leg.

The surface erupted and boiled around him. Pale deathly hands reached out to clutch at him and drag him under. The struggle was brief.

"Sedir had the key to the lock," Myrene said ruefully, "and I'm not going in after it."

They sat on the "sacrificial altar," still chained back-to-back. They had managed to use one of Sedir's knives to cut the ropes binding the boy who had been the intended sacrifice. He had then run on ahead to his village to tell family and friends the news of his rescue and the demise of Veidan Sedir in the Lake of Souls.

"The boy said his uncle was a blacksmith," Tiphane said, "and would break the chains."

"Do you think he'll remember to send him?" Myrene asked.

"I doubt it. They'll be celebrating all night."

Already, the autumn sun was making its westward descent. The Lake of Souls darkened in the shadows of the mountains.

"I'm cold," Tiphane said, "and hungry."

"Let's go before all the feasting is over."

"That village is five miles away, and over a mountain path, no less."

"Then we'd better get started."

Tiphane groaned.

They stood up, accustomed by now to coordinating their efforts.

"What about Cha'korth?" Myrene asked.

Tiphane glanced at the warrior still caught in the rapture of the ecstasy spell. "The spell will wear off in a day or so. Exposure to the harmony of Givean will undoubtedly give him a new perspective on the way he leads his life. Like it did for you."

Myrene snorted.

The two women sidled and shuffled along the trail that skirted the lake. It was slow going.

"Why is it again you can't magic these chains away?" Myrene asked.

"As I've told you, I am not a lockpick. I'm a—"

"I know, I know. A weaver of light and wind and rain. And your power can't touch worked iron."

"Exactly." Tiphane paused, then added, "I could accelerate the rusting of the iron so that it weakens and breaks."

"How long would that take?"

Tiphane sighed. "About a year."

"Just perfect."

Tiphane shrugged with a rattle of chains at the limitations of her magic.

"There is one positive thing that has come out of this," Myrene said.

Tiphane, of course, knew it was not only the demise of Veidan Sedir that made this a good day, but the reaffirmation of their friendship. So it surprised her when Myrene sniffed and said with great joy, "My head has never felt so clear!"

The eagle soared above the lake, anxious to tell his brothers and sisters all he had witnessed. Never before had he seen such sport, and he wondered what folly the winds held next for the two females. Whatever it was, it was sure to be entertaining.

Maybe, the eagle decided, he would stick around and find out.

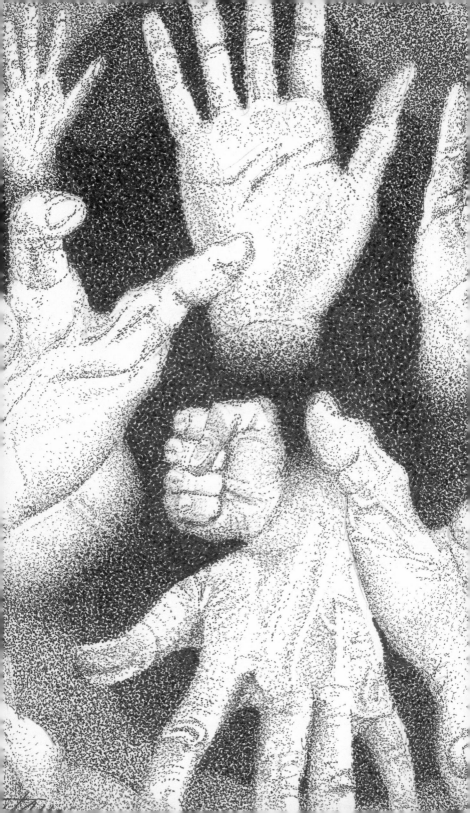

THE DREAM GATHERER

From *Karigan G'ladheon and the Green Riders: A History* by Lady Estral Andovian Fiori, the Golden Guardian of Selium

Vol. 2, Appx. B "Author Notes and Reminisces"
(3) The Berry Sisters, Seven Chimneys, the *Draugmkelder*

Among the first helpers Karigan encountered on that long-ago journey was a pair of elderly sisters improbably located in the wilds of the Green Cloak Forest. They were the daughters of one Professor Erasmus Norwood Berry, who had been an instructor at Selium. His interests lay in the arcane arts, but back then, such a field of study was anathema to the leadership of the school, including the then Golden Guardian. It is not surprising considering that the general populace of Sacoridia equated all magic with the evil of Mornhavon the Black, who had committed such terrible crimes during the Long War. Professor Berry was subsequently exiled from Selium and never set foot on the campus again. Despite his dismissal from the school, he continued his inquiries into the nature of magic from his estate in the Green Cloak. After his death, it seems his daughters inherited all, including his extensive library and myriad magical objects he had collected over the course of decades (notably, for this reminisce, a model ship-in-a-bottle, which, it turned out, was no model). His daughters did not continue his work, however, but resided quietly at the estate they called Seven Chimneys.

Penelope and Isabelle Berry, also known as Bunch Berry

and Bay Berry respectively (the sobriquets given them by their father after the local flora), took in the exhausted Karigan and made her warm, dry, and well-fed. Karigan spoke so vividly of these eccentric ladies, their hospitality, and their unusual home that I secretly hoped to one day meet them. When it finally happened, it couldn't have been at a better time . . .

The Dream Gatherer

Return to Seven Chimneys

"We have been away too long. Farnham will have his hands full."

Two sisters, clearly in their elder years and of gentle breeding, looked in dismay upon the grounds of their estate. Entire swaths of greenery had browned and died from an unnatural inland incursion of seawater and were only now starting to regreen. In other places, the forest encroached on the formerly well-kept lawns and gardens. Plantings that had once been carefully cultivated and groomed now grew in riotous abandon. Farnham, their groundskeeper, certainly would have his hands full.

The taller and frailer of the two sisters, attired in a dark-green velvet dress and leaning on a cane of twisted hickory, shook herself. "The grounds are not the first thing *I* see when I look upon our home. Is that what *you* see?"

"Well," the other mused—she was rather rounder of girth than her sister and favored the color of burnt orange with a crisp white apron. "The ship *does* add character to the house."

They stood in the drive beside a carriage burdened with trunks and parcels and furniture, with no evidence of horses or carriage driver or attendants to be seen.

"Honestly, Bunch," the one in green said, "I have never heard such understatement from you in all my years."

The home their father had built, a country manse of stone and timber, rose in the midst of the estate. Grand it was, or at least it had been. Peculiar, it now appeared, with the addition of a pirate ship protruding from its midsection. The figurehead of a mermaid seemed to stare at them in accusation.

"Perhaps we should rename the house Three Masts," Bunch suggested.

"Don't you dare," her sister, who went by Bay, countered. "Father named it Seven Chimneys, and so it shall always be known."

There were actually nine chimneys, or there had been until the ship's materialization had knocked one over. Others slanted at precarious angles. Their father, the late Professor Erasmus Norwood Berry, who had been a collector of arcane curios, had deemed the number seven far more magical than nine, and so bestowed the name "*Seven* Chimneys" upon the house. Whatever it was called, the masts towered above the roof, the slate tiles now neatly arranged around them as if the ship had been part of the house's original construction.

"I do believe birds are nesting on yon spars," Bay said, squinting.

"Oh, let us not start arguing about birds again."

"They *are* gulls. They do not belong, and their rookery is making an unacceptable mess of the roof."

"Never mind the roof," Bunch said. "Our front door seems to have been replaced by the bow of the ship. We will have to use the kitchen entrance."

The two slowly made their way along the drive, observing how, like the roof with the masts, the house had incorporated the ship into its structure by reassembling the masonry and timbers to hug the contours of the hull.

"A master craftsman could not have done better," Bunch said with admiration and pride.

Bay *hrrrumpfed*. "We'll see what it looks like on the inside."

As the sisters rounded the side of the house where the kitchen entrance awaited, the carriage they'd left behind, seemingly without the aid of horses or driver, rolled off toward the stables.

The sisters glanced at one another when they reached the kitchen door. Since there was no reason to lock a house out in the wilds of the Green Cloak Forest, Bay simply pushed the door open.

Bunch placed her hands over her eyes. "I do not know if I can bear to look."

"The house has mended its exterior," Bay replied, "as much as it can with the pirate ship, at any rate, but as for the interior?"

The two lingered on the threshold.

Bay took a sniff of the air that flowed out. "Has a briny tang to it, wouldn't you say?"

Bunch only moaned.

Holding onto one another, they stepped into the kitchen. Hazy light filtered through windows and fell upon tables and counters and cabinets, and the great cookstove. Pans gleamed dully from where they hung overhead. Debris crunched underfoot—broken dishes and bits of furniture and unidentifiable bric-a-brac that was evidence of the tide of seawater that had washed through the house when the thief Thursgad had broken the bottle with the ship in it.

"Letitia will be none too pleased," Bay said, a quaver in her voice.

"Oh, our poor things." Bunch picked a piece of broken

vase out of the debris. They'd rescued some of their belongings in the immediate aftermath, but certainly not all.

"Our house has mended itself but, alas, does not do the cleaning." Bay turned over the moldering pages of a book with the tip of her cane. "As hurtful as it is, these are just things."

"But mother's and father's treasures—"

"*Things,*" Bay insisted. "Their time is past. We've still the house itself, and I suspect not all is destroyed."

"That is oddly optimistic of you, Bay."

They made their way to the central hall, or where it was supposed to be, and were blocked floor to ceiling by the barnacle-speckled hull of the ship.

"I do not think Letitia will fancy cleaning the ship," Bunch said.

There was a wisp, like a puff of air, beside them that indicated that, indeed, Letitia did not fancy it at all.

"We will clean this place," Bay said, "and Farnham will cut doors through the hull so we can access all the house, but in the meantime, let us retire to the kitchen for tea. This all has been most distressing."

At that moment, a *thump* came from above and both sisters looked up, but there was only the ceiling.

"What do you suppose that was?" Bunch asked.

"I hope it is not the accursed squirrels making a domicile of our attic again," Bay replied. "The mess they made last time! If so, we'll have squirrel stew on the menu again." She did not look displeased by the prospect.

"That sounded larger than squirrels," Bunch said.

"Raccoons?"

"Bigger."

"Then you will have to take a look." Bay did not do stairs.

"*I* will not go crawling in that attic," Bunch declared.

They both turned and stared into space. A breath of air huffed into their faces.

"I believe," Bay said, "that Letitia does not plan on climbing into the attic either."

Over the days that followed, there were no more mysterious thumps from above, though the old house creaked and groaned in ways that were new to the sisters due to the addition of the ship. They threw themselves into cleanup and salvage, and Farnham cut doors through the hull of the ship, which allowed access through all parts of the house, but from which drafted the odor of dead fish and worse. All windows were left open whether it snowed, rained, or the sun shone.

The interior walls of the house had plastered and repainted themselves around the ship just as stone and timber had on the exterior, but the repairs did not intrude past the hull. So, inside the hull, the ship was a ship. It did, however, change the shape and size of some rooms in the house. Bunch was beside herself that there were portholes looking into her bed chamber, and the east gable guestroom now featured a jolly boat.

Decks were swabbed and the ship cleaned as best as could be. The detritus of the pirates was, fortunately, little, though Bay groused about the lack of treasure. She did claim a few scattered coins. Any other metal they found—a broken knife, a navigator's backstaff, anchor chains—was rusted. Anything that was leather or textile or paper was almost nonexistent, except for the sails and rigging. Even the waggoner, a book of charts depicting the known seas and a treasure of its own on any ship, looked . . . gnawed upon. Something had nibbled away most of the pages, and the cover, too. Oddly, the sisters found no evidence of rodents—unheard of on any ship.

"Raccoons." Bay picked up the tattered waggoner. "Raccoons chewed on it."

"It is not raccoons," Bunch replied. "Look here." A corner of a writing desk in the captain's cabin was marked unmistakably by the indentation of human teeth. "The pirates were starving."

Bay brightened. "Do you suppose they ate one another?"

"What an awful thought! Not at all proper for a lady. What would mother say?"

Working in the affected rooms of the house proved more difficult than the ship, for the sisters had to go through personal items, including those that had belonged to generations of the Berry family. Objects that could not be rescued—priceless rugs, artworks, furniture, pottery, and, worst of all, books—were sorrowfully consigned to rubbish heaps.

Their father's library, with all its rare books and artifacts of an arcane quality, was the place where the ship-in-a-bottle had been when it broke and caused the cataclysmic emergence of the pirate ship, along with a good deal of ocean and at least one flock of seagulls. The room took the brunt of the destruction and was weirdly melded with a lower deck of the ship, wood cladding twisting through plaster. In some places, shelves of books remained as if untouched. In others they were just piles of moldering pulp. Still others stuck halfway into the hull, the gold-leaf lettering on the spines glittering in the light.

Bunch brought baskets of the debris down to the parlor where Bay was sorting through some of their father's papers that had been water damaged. Bunch picked a dented brass tube out of the basket. "Oh, look," she said, "father's special telescope. The lenses are broken out of it, I'm afraid."

"Perhaps it is not entirely a bad thing," Bay replied. "Its visions were dangerous on occasion."

"True. As I've always said, it is never advisable to dabble with the past or future, but it was father's prized possession, so I am sad it is broken. His old harp is in splinters, too." Bunch picked up a mangled piece of wood, broken wire-wrapped gut strings hanging crazily in all directions. She sniffed. The glistening of a tear filled her eye. "I shall miss the music, but perhaps the voices of the strings are finally free."

"You are getting much too maudlin, sister." Bay set aside the papers and started sifting through the basket with the tip of her cane.

Bunch pulled a handkerchief from her sleeve and dabbed her eyes. "I can't help it. All the devastation, all of our things."

"Not everything," Bay reminded her. "What we need—" Her cane scuffed against something metallic. "What's this?" She nudged the object again, then bent to investigate.

"What?" Bunch asked.

"Eh?"

"You were saying what it was that we needed."

"Yeees, right. What we need is a party to celebrate our return to Seven Chimneys."

Bunch clapped her hands. "That is a fine idea." Then she sobered. "But we are alone out here. How will we ever get anyone to attend?"

Bay tugged the object she'd been inspecting out of the debris and raised it for Bunch to see. "This might help." It was a tin lantern pierced with the design of constellations.

"Father's *draugmkelder*? It survived?"

"It seems it has," Bay replied. "Not even rusted. Now we can invite as many guests as we wish."

Bunch gazed at the lantern with trepidation. "But gathering dreams can be perilous."

Bay gave her sister a catlike smile. "And amusing."

A thud from above gave them both a start. Bay rapped the ceiling with her cane. This was followed by a scurrying sound and she rapped the ceiling again—*bang-bang-bang!*

"I *will* have my squirrel stew! I *will!*"

"Or perhaps," Bunch mused, "our first guest."

Stickles

When it came to Letitia's attention that some items had gone missing from the larder, she made the situation plain to the sisters. It was clear that the thumps and bumps they heard from above were not produced by squirrels or raccoons. Together they devised a trap for their "guest." They left the remains of dinner in the kitchen, a roast fowl, a jar of pickled herring, a slab of cheese, and a dish of bread pudding. The sisters hid in Bay's bedchamber, which was near the kitchen. They left the lamp turned down and a pot of tea at their disposal, and played Trickits to pass the time. They were at pains to place the wooden tiles down as quietly as possible so as not to tip off the thief.

"How will we know when our food pilferer snatches the bait?" Bay asked.

"I believe Letitia will ensure we are aware."

As the night wore on and the pot of tea cooled, Bay snored in her chair and Bunch dozed over the unfinished game of Trickits. A scream abruptly caused Bay to knock her cane against their tea table, clattering the service, which in turn caused Bunch to jump to her feet with her hand over her heart.

"Gracious," she said breathlessly, "I think that is our culprit."

The two hobbled to the kitchen as fast as they could, Bunch carrying a lamp. When they arrived, the lamplight revealed a skillet hurtling through the air after a man who ran around in circles in an effort to escape it.

"Even after all these years," Bay said, her gaze following the action, "I will never get over seeing, or not seeing if you take my meaning, Letitia wielding cookware."

The man glanced over his shoulder and screamed again. The skillet flashed down and clanged him on his head. The scream was cut short, and he wobbled on his feet before spiraling to a heap on the floor.

The skillet then clattered onto a sideboard.

"Well done, Letitia dear," Bunch said. She brightened the lamp so they could see the man better.

"He is a very large squirrel," Bay said. "We'll need a huge pot."

"Now don't be silly, Bay."

The fellow was not much to look at. He was skinny with a long, narrow face. Hair straggled like seaweed from beneath his stocking cap, and he wore the garb of a disreputable pirate—a loose dirty shirt and baggy pants, and most damning of all, nothing on his feet.

"My," Bay said, waving the air before her, "but he does smell most inappropriate."

"That is putting it mildly. I thought all the pirates were slain."

"We were misinformed as it is clear they were not. The question is, what do we do with this one now that we have him? Aside from finding a large enough pot to stew him in, that is."

"You are being silly again, sister. Let us send Letitia for Farnham and Rolph for assistance."

The trouble with invisible servants was never knowing their location and if they heard what was desired of them, but when the kitchen door swung open and closed seemingly of its own accord, the sisters assumed it was Letitia heading out to fetch Farnham and Rolph.

Bay peered down at their pirate once more. "Is that a barnacle on his chin?"

After the pirate had come to, he was told in no uncertain terms that he must bathe before tea.

"Tea?"

"Are you slow, Sir Pirate?" Bay asked, her voice nasal from pinching her nose closed against the stench. "Of course, tea."

"Patience, sister," Bunch said. "Letitia did wallop him on the head quite hard. It may have rattled his brain."

After he got over his initial confusion, he said, "But bathing more than once a year isn't good for you. It's bad luck—everyone knows that."

"Then we shall turn you out," Bay said.

Much to their surprise, the pirate acquiesced. He reluctantly agreed to let Rolph and Farnham lead him to the bathing room where they scrubbed him down. The sisters listened at the door to water gushing and splashing, and the pirate blubbering and *gah*ing.

After the bath, Farnham cropped the pirate's hair to his scalp. It had consisted in large part, as it turned out, of seaweed to which periwinkles and dog whelks clung. The sisters gave him some of Professor Berry's old clothes to wear, his own being burned in the fire. He seemed not to know how to walk with shoes on, and the professor's smoking jacket hung from him as though he were a scarecrow. Even though the barnacle still adhered to his chin, he smelled, much to the relief of the sisters, acceptable.

They bade him sit with them. If they feared the pirate would go rabid on them, they were reassured by the skillet that hovered in the air behind him. He, on the other hand, did not appear reassured. He kept glancing over his shoulder. With questioning, they learned his name was Stickles, which disappointed Bay who wanted to call him Barney because of the barnacle.

"Master Stickles," Bunch said as she poured him a cup of tea, "tell us what position you held on the ship."

"Just a lowly hand, ma'am. Did whatever I was told." He took the cup into weatherworn hands and held it like it was a foreign object, which it undoubtedly was to him.

Bunch offered him a plate of dainties. It was late for tea, this being the middle of the night, but Bunch had declared it was never too late to be civilized.

When he did not reach for any of the dainties, Bay said, "You're not going to have any? You seemed perfectly willing to relieve us of our other food."

"Uh," Stickles said, "I am woozy since your ghost knocked my head." He took another anxious look over his shoulder. "Rum might wash it down."

Bunch shook her head. "Master Stickles, for one, Letitia is beyond a doubt in the land of the living, and for two, we run a good decent household. This is no unruly pirate den of miscreancy. You will find no demon rum here."

He gazed mournfully into his teacup. "I'm real sorry about taking your food. Y'see, we didn't have much to eat on the ship, me and the other fellows."

"Did you eat the other fellows?" Bay asked eagerly.

He just stared at her with wide eyes.

"*Bay!*" Bunch cleared her throat. "Now Master Stickles,

about those others. They left, went out into the wide world. Why did you remain behind?"

"I thought they were crazy to leave," he declared. "I mean, look at this place. Nicer than anything I've ever seen—even better than Madam Salas's bawdy house on Helos Harbor." At the sisters' looks of disapproval and the rapid approach of the skillet, he hastily added, "Er, sorry, meaning no disrespect, ma'ams. I did not mean to suggest . . . " He licked his lips. ". . . to compare this fine manse to a bawdy house."

"Go on," Bay said tersely.

"Well, your nice house was one reason I stayed, and my ship the other. The *Mermaid's* about all I've known for many years and I couldn't leave her, especially now that she's land-locked and has doorways carved in her." Crinkles formed across his forehead. "That's cruel for such a grand ship."

"We are not exactly pleased to have a ship in our house," Bunch said. "It has been something of a *disruption*."

"To say the least," Bay agreed. "So you say you stayed behind despite the decision of your shipmates to venture forth."

Stickles nodded. "I couldn't abandon the *Mermaid*, and—and the pantry was stocked and so—"

"*Was*," Bay said. "We had to go to lengths to refill it."

The skillet hovered menacingly.

Sweat slipped down Stickles's face. He cleared his throat. "Sorry."

Silence filled the room and Stickles seemed to sink into himself. After what seemed an eternity, Bay told her sister, "He is fairly well spoken for a pirate."

"Fairly, and seemingly honest at that."

"Not as heathenish as one might expect."

Stickles glanced back and forth from one sister to the

other. They stared directly at him as if they'd come to some unvoiced conclusion.

"We understand your ship was your home," Bunch told him, "as you must understand this house is ours."

"Yes," Bay said. "My sister and I shall keep you."

"*Keep* me?" More sweat glistened on his forehead.

"What my sister means to say," Bunch told him, "is that we shall keep you on. Like a deckhand. We'll feed you and not turn you away from your ship. In return, we expect some assistance around the house. But there will be *no* rum."

Bay nodded solemnly. "Indeed. We are also planning a celebration for which you will help us prepare."

"In the meantime," Bunch said, "do you play Trickits?"

"Or perhaps," Bay said, stroking the handle of her cane, "Intrigue?"

The Golden Guardian

The unrelenting rain and clouds turned day to night beneath the eaves of the Green Cloak Forest where a group of sodden travelers rode down the North Road heading south and west on their way to the city of Selium. Hoods were drawn and shoulders slumped against the weather. Estral Andovian, now the Lady Fiori and Golden Guardian of Selium, rode up front with Lieutenant Rennard of the River Unit. Seven of his soldiers followed, one riding the near horse that hauled the field carriage with its somber burden. Spared from duty in the north following the Battle of the Lone Forest, the soldiers formed an honor guard for Estral's father who'd been slain in the fighting. His rough pine casket borne upon the field carriage was shrouded in an oilskin tarp against the wet.

Estral's initial shock over her father's death had waned over the long days of travel and turned into a mire of despair. She barely noticed the passage of time and simply went through the motions of her daily routine. Rennard had tried to engage her in conversation and include her in decisions, but she'd taken little interest and now he mostly left her alone. Left her alone to stew in her own dark thoughts about how she should have tried harder to dissuade her father from joining in the battle, how her own actions caused her best friend to be captured by the enemy and tortured. These things cut through her mind in a relentless agony that she embraced.

"Lieutenant!" one of the men called.

"What is it?" Rennard reined his horse around.

Estral halted Coda.

"I think we picked up a stone," the soldier said. "I need to stop and take a look." He dismounted and lifted his horse's hoof.

Not sure why she did so, Estral squeezed Coda forward instead of waiting.

"Lady Fiori," Rennard called, "you should not leave the group."

"Not going far," she said in a weak, scratchy voice. She was surprised it worked at all when so often she had to resort to using her slate and chalk to "speak."

He did not stop her for he had turned his attention to examining the horse's hoof. Truth be told, she'd been hungering to be alone, away from Rennard and his soldiers with their eyes on her all the time; away from the box that held her father, a constant reminder of her failures and guilt.

As Coda plodded along, she did not stop him as she had indicated to Rennard that she would. She glanced over her shoulder and saw that the honor guard had already vanished behind a bend in the road. Even knowing they would catch up with her in no time, she felt an easing, as though shackles had fallen from her wrists.

She'd an urge to apply her heels to Coda's sides and fly to unknown destinations, to run away from responsibility, but she hadn't the courage. Her path was clear. With her father gone, she was now the Golden Guardian of Selium, an inherited title not unlike that of a lord-governor. The Golden Guardian, however, did not oversee a province, but the history, culture, and arts of Sacoridia, as well as the school at Selium and the city itself. Fortunately, others handled most of the day-to-day management of school and city, but still it weighed on her. She might have filled in for her father when he was off on one of his many journeys, so she was prepared in a practical manner, but now she must bear the full burden of the office, including its politics. She would no longer be the Golden Guardian's daughter who only wanted to teach music to children, but the Golden Guardian who must weather the storms of decision-making vital to the well-being of Sacoridia's culture, and to Selium's students, instructors, and citizens.

The rain fell heavier and a fog thickened in the woods and billowed across the road. It was like a physical manifestation of how she felt inside—gray and clouded. She sank deep into thought, lulled by the rhythm of Coda's easygoing stride. So submerged was she, her mind going everywhere and nowhere, that when she shook herself back to the present she wasn't sure how much time had passed, and realized, with surprise, the honor guard had not caught up with her. She reined Coda around thinking she ought to ride back to meet them, but where was the road? How had she gotten off track? She wheeled the gelding around again, but there was no sign of it in any direction.

After a moment of panic, she thought, *It has to be nearby. The fog is just hiding it.*

She prodded Coda in a widening circle, but when they did not encounter the road, her panic intensified. Then she spotted a brighter patch of fog clear of trees in one direction and decided that had to be it, but when she crossed into the bright patch, she found herself on a narrow path, not the road. The path was well-tended, the gravel of the treadway raked. The forest fell away in a more orderly manner than the usual wildness of the Green Cloak. The underbrush and snags had been cleared away making the woods look neat. Bunchberry flowers grew in profusion close to the ground in a white mat beneath the emerald boughs of the woods.

She might have lost the North Road, but she was relieved to have found some sign of civilization. Chances were there was a house at the end of the path and its inhabitants could direct her back to the road. The fog thinned as she guided Coda along the path, which widened enough for two carriages to pass. Coda's hooves clip-clopped over a stone bridge that spanned a pleasant burbling stream. She halted him on the other side so she could absorb, in wonder, an open park-like area where the forest gave way to manicured lawns that in the distance faded in a light fog. The gold haze of the sun settled like an enchantment upon the grass and plantings. It was so unexpected here in the—

A man burst out from the shrubbery, screaming and waving some sort of a weapon at her. Coda reared. She tumbled off his back into bushes beside the stream and watched in dismay as her horse, with all her belongings, bolted back toward the fog. She fought herself free of the bushes, bayberry by the scent of the crushed foliage, to confront her assailant.

He shoved his weapon in her face. It was not a sword or a pike, not even a staff, but a rake. One look at the man suggested a scarecrow. He practically swam in too-large clothes and wore a straw hat that shaded his long face. And was that a barnacle on his chin?

"Don't you move," he said.

She knew a rake could cause damage. Uprisings had been won with such implements. She did not move though she was anxious to catch Coda. Hoping her voice would work, she

White "petals" are **bracts.** Flowers are actually located in the center of the bract formation.

Bunchberry

Member of the dogwood family. Diminutive white flowers in summer.

Clusters of orange-red berries in late summer.

fig. 1

Bayberry

Glossy, dark green summer foliage; small, waxy berries used in candle making.

figs. 2

K. Brutan

cleared her throat and said, "I will not move, but now what?" To her surprise, her voice worked better than it had in weeks. It sounded almost normal.

The man scratched his head beneath his hat. "Uh . . . "

"Look," Estral said, "I just wanted to ask directions on how to get back to the North Road and now you've scared off my horse."

He scratched his head again. "Uh . . . "

"Well? Are you just going to make me stand here all day?"

"Uh, no. I guess I'll take you to see my mistresses. They can decide what to do with you."

She hoped these mistresses of his would sort out the whole thing, and that she'd be able to retrieve Coda afterward. When the fog unveiled a large house in the distance, she could hardly believe it. To the man's consternation, she raced ahead.

The Benevolence of the House

"Wait!" the fellow cried, sprinting after Estral with his rake in hand.

Estral barely heard him as she'd started laughing, and she didn't stop until she came under the shadow of the ship's prow that split the covered front porch of the manse in two. She gazed upon it in wonder.

It can't be, can it?

The man skidded to a stop. He then approached with mincing footfalls like a cat that has stepped in something disagreeable. The problem appeared to be his boots.

"This isn't," she said, "Seven Chimneys, is it? Home of the Berry sisters?"

He puffed his chest out. "And Deckhand Stickles."

It had been, she supposed, a silly question to ask. After all, how many manor houses were there in the wilds of the Green Cloak with a ship protruding from them? She supposed it was possible there were others, but she'd only heard of one, and that from her friend Karigan. At the time of Karigan's visit with the Berry sisters some five years ago, however, there had been no ship, or it had been, at least, still contained in its bottle. It was later, from a copy of testimony given by a book thief named Thursgad, that she'd read about the ship part. Those who'd taken the testimony had, she learned, been skeptical. Even as she gazed upon the house and ship, she could hardly believe it herself.

77

The sensation of someone watching her drew her eyes upward to settle on the figurehead of a mermaid, its curved fish tail of fins and scales carved in detail, the human part of her lovingly crafted, the pale skin, her ruby lips, and wild red hair. She did not cast her gaze down on Estral, but seemed to look infinitely out upon the horizon, which must have been very appropriate at sea, but now all that lay before her was the vastness of the lawn, and beyond that, the forest. The ocean was very far away.

"My mistresses are in the back garden," Deckhand Stickles said. He gestured vaguely with the rake and held it ready in an offensive position.

"Were you on the ship when it—" She gave a vague wave of her hand toward the bow.

He nodded, a wary look in his eye.

"That is amazing! You must tell me all about it!"

Then, before his surprised gaze, she set off in the direction he'd indicated at an eager pace. She could not wait to meet the Berry sisters.

As they rounded the house, she spotted various outbuildings, including stables and a carriage house. Far down the back lawn, set among a copse of trees behind a pond, was what she guessed to be a garden folly with a spired rooftop poking above the canopy. She turned, and there immediately behind the house stood three figures dwarfed by the stern of the ship. She hurried toward them, barely aware of Stickles and his rake behind her.

She halted at the edge of fresh-turned earth and stared at them, and they stared back. The sisters were just as Karigan had described them, one tall and thin with a sharp countenance—that was Miss Bay—and the other plump and more prone to smiling—Miss Bunch. Both had blueberry-blue eyes set in crinkled elfin faces. The third figure turned out to be a statue of an old woman with birdseed cupped in her hand—Marin the Gardener, Estral surmised, in her crone's visage. Yellow roses climbed up her torso. The ship's anchor had been dropped and sat embedded in the ground next to the statue as if it had just missed crushing it. Roses had begun to wrap around it as well. So tickled was Estral to see the Berry sisters that a laugh escaped her throat unbidden.

"Stickles," Miss Bunch said, "have you brought us a guest?"

"An intruder," he said. "She is my prisoner."

"Stickles," Miss Bay said, "put that rake down immediately. This is not a pirate ship and threatening visitors with rakes is not courteous behavior."

"But—"

Under Miss Bay's stern gaze, he relented and dropped the rake head to the ground.

"It is certainly not how we treat the Golden Guardian of Selium," Miss Bunch said.

"How do you know who I am?" Estral asked.

Miss Bunch smiled as if addressing a particularly dense child. "Your harp badge is one clue."

Estral's hand went reflexively to the brooch pinned to her coat. It had been her father's, the ancient symbol of the minstrels, this one heavier and embellished with script in Old Sacoridian that read, *Serve Knowledge*. Few would have been able to distinguish it from an average minstrel's badge, though it had a weight and patina of age about it that suggested it was more.

"It is also difficult to miss your Eletian blood," Miss Bay added. "There are not likely to be others who are also minstrels."

Her Eletian blood was not difficult to miss? The only others who had ever recognized it were Eletians.

"We had some tidings," Miss Bunch said, "of what befell your father. We are truly sorry for your loss."

"But how—?" It had happened only recently in the far reaches of the north. How could they have heard about it already?

"Now and then we acquire the news of the land," Miss Bunch replied, "but gracious, Bay, I do not think it is polite to leave our guest gaping here by the garden plot. And Stickles, you must get back to work."

"My companions," Estral said, not without some reluctance, "are back on the North Road. I should get back to them."

"Nonsense," Miss Bay said. "They will be just fine without you for a little while. We would be remiss to not offer you our hospitality."

"But they'll be worried."

"They will hardly notice your absence." Miss Bunch patted her arm.

An indefinable feeling told Estral this was true.

"And of course you must join us for the party," Miss Bunch continued.

"Party?"

"Tonight!" Miss Bay answered. "You are our first guest. Well, second if you count Stickles."

More than a little flummoxed, Estral could only relent when the sisters each took her by the arm, one to either side of her, and gently guided her around the house. They chattered almost continuously, sometimes nonsensically, as they led Estral to a side door with a trellis cloaked in more climbing roses. There seemed to be an ongoing disagreement about birds.

"They are *sea*gulls," Miss Bay insisted. "As such, they belong in the *sea,* not whitewashing our roof."

"Now, sister, you *see* gulls everywhere." Miss Bunch said.

"That is because they *are* everywhere!"

Estral looked up and did notice some herring gulls on the peak of the roof.

They entered the kitchen.

"Letitia," Miss Bunch sang out, "please put some tea on. A guest has arrived!"

Estral smiled to herself for Letitia, she knew, was one of the sisters' invisible servants. According to Karigan, they had all been banished to invisibility and silence by a spell of Professor Berry's that had gone awry. She realized it had been a long time since she had smiled so much. Too long, but there had been reasons.

Reaching the parlor required passing through the hull of the ship, which was dank and gloomy compared to the non-ship parts of the house with its leaded windows. A wooden walkway with a handrail had been built to traverse the hold, over piles of stone ballast that might otherwise be difficult terrain for two elderly ladies to cross. Estral held her breath against the stench of bilge and mold and long-dead sea creatures. It was a sticky smell, the sort that clung to you like a limpet. On the other side, the parlor itself appeared truncated by the hull, upon which the sisters had hung paintings of flowers in vases and bowls of fruit as if to negate the presence of the ship in their house. The bilge stench followed them into the room. Whether the sisters were in denial about the ship or not, the lingering smell made it pretty hard to forget. Lace curtains tousled in open windows, and the fresh breezes did help to diminish the smell some.

As though Letitia had anticipated the sisters' desire, a tea service and a plate of pound cake awaited them on a table. They seated themselves and Miss Bunch poured.

"Your arrival is quite auspicious," she said.

81

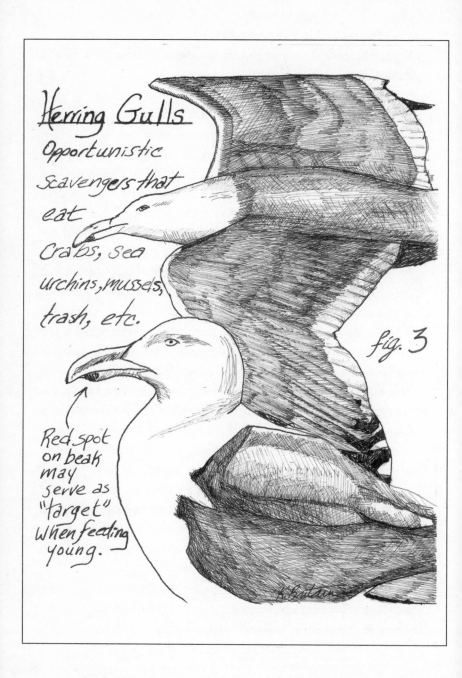

Estral was so busy trying to take it all in—the sisters, the ship, the parlor—that it was a moment before she realized she had been spoken to.

"Why is that?" she asked.

"Why, our party, child. We are so happy to have you here to join in our celebration commemorating our return to our house. We were gone so long while it mended itself that we must celebrate our homecoming."

"And our escape from Miss Poppy," Miss Bay muttered.

"Our cousin down south," Miss Bunch told Estral, "with whom we stayed while we were unhoused. She is, shall we say, difficult."

"Disagreeable," Miss Bay amended.

"Now, sister, we must not be unkind. She put a roof over our heads when we needed it."

Miss Bay *hrrrumphed,* then spooned two lumps of sugar into her tea. "We do not get visitors often so we are very glad you stopped by." It was said as if Estral had intentionally just dropped in for a casual visit. Miss Bay reached for the cream, but Miss Bunch pulled it out of her reach with a look of remonstration. Miss Bay frowned.

"Remember your delicate internal constitution," Miss Bunch said.

Miss Bay grumbled unintelligibly.

"I am very excited to have found you," Estral told them. "My friend Karigan told me all about you."

"That makes us sound famous," Miss Bunch said, using the cream she'd denied her sister.

"Karigan *who*?" Miss Bay asked. "What a funny name."

"Don't you remember her?" Estral asked. "She visited with you a few years ago."

"I remember," Miss Bunch said, "and so do you, sister. She was the Green Rider who was not, who really was."

Miss Bay bobbed her eyebrows and sipped her tea.

"You gave her the moonstone," Estral said.

"Oh, that old thing," said Miss Bunch. "I'd almost forgotten."

Estral had a sense that neither of the ladies had forgotten a thing.

"Tell us what our Karigan has been up to since we last saw her," Miss Bunch said, "though we may have some idea."

She didn't doubt they had "some idea." They waited for her to begin with beatific smiles on their faces. As eccentric as they seemed nattering on about seagulls, she could see in their eyes an intensity of regard, a sharp canniness, and it made her shiver a little.

"Well . . . " She hesitated. On the journey north, she'd begun writing about the Green Riders in general, and Karigan in particular, so there was plenty to speak about, but she'd another concern.

"What is it, child?" Miss Bunch inquired.

"My voice," she replied. "It's remarkably good at the moment, but it may not hold."

Both sisters gazed at her as if in understanding.

"There is a spell in you that stole your voice, yes?" Miss Bay asked.

"How do you know?"

"We *know*. We know in a similar way that you know things about us," Miss Bay said.

"And we are our father's daughters," Miss Bunch added.

Estral waited for more, but it seemed they were not going to give her a full explanation. "If you are so well-informed, then you do not need me to tell you about Karigan."

To her surprise, Miss Bunch chuckled and said to her sister, "She *is* the Fiori."

Miss Bay responded with a thin smile.

What, Estral wondered, was *that* supposed to mean?

"Dear child," Miss Bunch said, "it is more that *you* need to tell us, is it not?"

Estral started.

"Indeed," Miss Bay agreed, "but we do enjoy tales, and no, we do not know *everything*. We will learn much from what you tell us."

"And do not worry about your voice," Miss Bunch added. "You are at Seven Chimneys and that spell has no effect here."

"It doesn't? Can—can you fix my voice permanently? Get rid of the spell?"

"No, child, that is not within our power. Seven Chimneys is really but an island, and once you leave our borders your voice will be what it has been and the spell will reassert its influence. I am truly sorry."

"Consider your ability to speak now," Miss Bay said, "a product of the benevolence of the house."

The benevolence of the house. The house had mended itself, they had said. It was not the first time she'd encountered inexplicable phenomena of a magical nature. In fact, her father had had a gift for it himself, if a subtle one. It had to do with the Fiori bloodline and the office of the Golden Guardian. As she assumed the mantle of Golden Guardian, she wondered what surprises awaited her.

In the meantime, she decided to simply accept that Seven Chimneys and the sisters were extraordinary, and so she began telling the tales of Karigan's adventures.

Doing the Right Thing

Estral began Karigan's story with events that followed her stay at Seven Chimneys, and recounted her adventures over the years, but stopped before describing the most recent that had taken place in the north. Her tea had gone cold by the time she took a sip to moisten her throat. It felt wonderful to have her whole voice again, but so much talking was exhausting. She was not used to it anymore. She glanced out the windows and was surprised to see that the daylight had changed little though she felt like she'd been talking for hours.

"Our Karigan is a plucky one," Miss Bunch said.

"And lucky," Miss Bay added.

"I am afraid there are details I lack," Estral said. "Karigan is not the most forthcoming about these things."

"Regardless," Miss Bunch said, "you have woven quite a tale of daring rescues, fierce battles, magic, and time travel, but if I'm not mistaken, there is much more."

"About what happened in the north," Miss Bay put in.

Estral gazed into her cold tea. Cream had turned it opaque. "That is harder to tell."

"Which makes it more important to have it out," Miss Bay said.

After a couple more sips, Estral resumed telling the sisters of journeying to the north with Karigan and their Eletian guide, Enver—she, to find her father who had gone missing;

Karigan and Enver, to find the p'ehdrosians, a race of part-human, part-moose people who'd been allies with Sacoridia during the Long War but then vanished from history.

When finally she reached the point in the story in which she, desperate to find her father, brashly ran off to the enemy-infested Lone Forest, she stumbled to a stop and cast her gaze down.

"What is it, child?" Miss Bunch asked.

"It's all my fault."

"What is?"

"Everything that followed." She shook her head and set the teacup on the table with a clink, then stood, stretched, and went over to one of the windows. She breathed deep of the fresh air perfumed by the scents of recent rain and ever-greens, and gazed at the pleasant view. Not far off, a rabbit nibbled on a shrub. She watched in surprise as Stickles entered the pastoral scene, taking careful, slow steps in his bare feet. He was clearly stalking the rabbit, his rake ready at hand to dispatch it. She was about to shout out to spook the rabbit, but as Stickles closed in, it sensed his presence and bounded away. Stickles watched after it, then bowed his head in defeat. She, in turn, closed her eyes in relief at the rabbit's escape.

"You were telling us about the Lone Forest, child," Miss Bunch reminded her.

"Which you ran into even though it was occupied by the enemy," Miss Bay added.

"*Second Empire,*" Miss Bunch provided.

"I *know.* What kind of imbecilic name is 'Second Empire' anyway?"

"I am sure it sounds just fine to *them.* Please continue, child."

With a heavy sigh, she resumed her narrative without looking at the sisters, without really seeing anything, not even the view out the window. "Second Empire had set traps throughout the forest and I got caught in one, a net that enclosed me like a purse and left me strung in a tree. Of course Karigan came looking for me even though she'd been ill."

Estral related how Karigan also managed to step into a trap and how they both then became prisoners of Second Empire. She forced herself to speak of Karigan's torture, the vicious flogging that had almost taken her life. By the time Estral finished, she was shaking. When she returned to her place on the sofa, Miss Bunch wrapped a throw around her shoulders. Shadows had lengthened outside and deepened in the room. Birds fluted and chirped an evensong.

"I am going to refresh our pot of tea," Miss Bunch declared. "Our guest dearly needs a hot cup."

Estral sat with her face in her hands. When she looked up, she found Miss Bay staring hard at her, which only confirmed her guilt and made her feel even worse. An uncomfortable silence built in the room and lingered for what felt like hours until Miss Bunch finally returned. Estral's relief was palpable. She accepted a fresh cup of tea sweetened with honey for her throat and sipped till it was all gone. It was a welcome distraction from the difficulty of her tale.

"Now tell us the rest," Miss Bunch said. "Tell us how you escaped and what transpired after."

Estral did, though it wasn't any easier than what had preceded it. She spoke of how Enver and a pair of gryphons saved her and Karigan, and how Karigan and Enver returned to the Lone Forest to rescue her father and King Zachary, who were also captives of Second Empire. The guilt weighed on her even more as she described the darkness and hopelessness Karigan fell into after all the torture and pain. They'd thought they'd lose her to it, but she rallied.

She finished with what she knew of the Battle of the Lone Forest and her father's death. By now the tears were a torrent. "He might be alive but for me."

Miss Bay banged the handle of her cane on the table and Estral jumped.

"What is this blubbering about everything being *your* fault?" the elder woman demanded.

Estral sniffed. "If my father hadn't joined the battle, he wouldn't have been killed. He went because he wanted to find the one who stole my voice."

The cane crashed on the table again and the tea service clattered.

"Sister," Miss Bunch said, "mind mother's fine porcelain . . . "

"Irrelevant! The child thinks she is responsible for the actions of all others."

"But—" Estral began.

"Did you cause your voice to be stolen?"

"Uh, no . . . "

"It is the thief's fault your voice went missing in the first place. And was your father not a being of free will?"

"What? I—"

"Enough!" Miss Bay's cane threatened to slam on the table again. "He chose to do many dangerous things during his lifetime, yes? And he chose these things knowing full well the possible consequences. It was not *your* doing, girl."

Estral was about to protest, but Miss Bay's penetrating gaze made her close her mouth.

"Do you mean to tell us," Miss Bay continued, "that your

father was stupid, that he went into the battle unthinking and oblivious?"

Estral shook her head. He was a seasoned fighter and the smartest person she knew. The last thing he was, was oblivious.

"He was a wise man, child," Miss Bunch said in a kinder tone than her sister. "He'd lived a long life and was very experienced with dangerous situations. Alas, it didn't help him in the end, but he certainly did not enter that situation blind. Recovering your voice may have been part of what motivated him, but do you think he would have stayed behind had it not been an issue?"

Estral slowly shook her head. No, he would not have been left behind. He would have joined his king and countrymen to fight the enemy, no matter what. "He'd do what he considered the right thing."

The sisters nodded in approval.

"As for our Karigan," Miss Bay said, "she made the same mistake as you."

Estral looked up. "Mistake? Karigan?"

"Yes. She made the mistake of caring too much for her friend and rushed into danger on her own. Perhaps if she had awaited the Eletian and taken a more cautious approach, she'd have been spared much grief. But no, she ran in just as you had. Still, just as your father knew the risks, she as a Green Rider would have been just as well aware of the dangers. That says much about how deeply she cares for you. Such friendship is a rare gift.

"Aside from her concern for your welfare, why do you think she followed you into the forest? Why do you think she engaged in any number of the heroic deeds you just recounted?"

She's mad, Estral wanted to say. *She's a Green Rider, it's what they do.* But she only shrugged.

"What is it you said about your father doing the right thing? She likely considered trying to rescue her friend the right thing to do, as well. Only in the aftermath can we judge her actions as perhaps foolhardy, but we weren't there in her boots weighing the options at hand, just as we were not in *yours.*"

"Child," Miss Bunch said, "you were desperate to find your father. That desperation may have overridden common sense, but it is understandable, and it was brave of you to have set out on your own. And dare I say, you thought you, too, were doing the right thing."

"I don't know what I was thinking," Estral muttered.

"You were thinking to find your father."

"If things had gone differently," Miss Bay said, "who is to say Karigan would have discovered your father and the king being held by Second Empire? What might have become of our king?"

"I have had all these thoughts and more," Estral said. "All the what-ifs. But no matter the logic or justification, I do not think I'll ever accept what happened."

"You know why, do you not?" Miss Bay asked. "Because you are human. You care about Karigan and loved your father. His death is a huge loss. Not to mention you suffered much at the hands of the torturers yourself when they forced you to witness what they did to Karigan. You will live with it all your life, but time and distance will mend the immediacy of it if not the fact."

Estral wiped the last of the tears away with her sleeve. She had accepted that it was her punishment to remember and relive those awful experiences, but the words of the Berry sisters did bring her some solace, if not healing. Healing would take time. Outside the window dusk had finally fallen.

Miss Bunch followed her gaze and announced, "It is time that we turned our sorrows to celebration—it is almost time."

"Time? For what?"

"The party, of course. We will proceed over to the folly. And let us not forget the draugmkelder, Bay."

The Draugmkelder

Before Estral could wonder too much about what a draugmkelder was, the sisters sent her in search of Stickles to tell him
it was time to go over to the party.

"Most likely you'll find him in front of the boat," Miss
Bunch said.

"The *bow* of the *ship*," Miss Bay corrected. "And he's
probably talking to the mermaid."

Or maybe stalking some poor bunny rabbits.

Estral made her way through the kitchen which was hot
with all the ovens afire. The aromas of roasting meat and
baking bread made her mouth water. Pies cooled on the sideboard. Letitia had been busy. Estral wondered if this was *all*
for the party. The sisters must be expecting a large turnout.
She didn't know where the other guests were coming from
considering the location, but maybe they had neighbors
tucked away nearby in the woods. Whatever the case, any
acquaintances of the Berry sisters were bound to be interest-
ing, and she was looking forward to meeting them. It would
be a good diversion, she thought, to take her mind off the
darkness of the events she had just relived for the sisters.

Outside it was pleasantly cool after the heat of the kitchen.
The sun was leaving behind splashes of peach in the sky. She
walked around to the front of the house, dew collecting on
her boots, and indeed found Stickles at the bow of the ship

93

gazing up at the figurehead. It appeared he'd dug up turf around the hull and had prepared it for planting.

"Hello," she said. He jumped. "Sorry, I didn't mean to startle you."

He wiped his hands on a rag. "It's all right," he mumbled.

She gazed at the mermaid. The waning backsplash of sunset gave the scales of her tail an iridescence, and the shifting shadows lent her life. "She's beautiful."

"Aye," he said, and that was all. He was not a pirate of many words.

"The sisters would like you to finish up so we can all go over to the party together, that is after you have—" and here Estral did a reasonable impression of Miss Bay, "—completed your ablutions and rendered yourself odorless. They also insist you wear shoes."

He simply grunted and bent to pick up his tools, grasping them with his knobby-knuckled fingers.

"Making a garden?" she asked.

"Aye, for *her*." He nodded toward the figurehead. "She's landlocked so least I can do is plant a garden for her."

"What does a pirate know about gardens?"

"Wasn't always a pirate. Grew up on a farm." He then turned and walked off with his tools toward one of the outbuildings that appeared to be a potting shed. She wondered briefly how he'd ended up a pirate, but figured it must have happened in the usual way, that he'd been gangpressed or otherwise stolen from whatever life he'd been living. She glanced once more at the figurehead now cloaked in shadow, shrugged, and headed back toward the kitchen entrance.

Fig. 4 <u>Firefly</u>

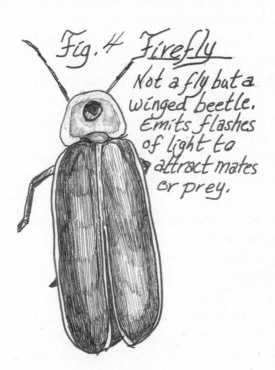

Not a fly but a winged beetle. Emits flashes of light to attract mates or prey.

The Firefly's "lamp"

K. Brotan

When finally everyone was ready and Stickles was even wearing shoes, Miss Bunch said, "Let us commence to the folly."

They filed out of the house, an unlit tin lantern swinging in Miss Bay's hand, and followed a path across the back lawn toward the pond and folly. The way was illuminated by fairy lights, little flames flickering along the path, among the branches of trees, and floating on the pond. A stone wall and boxwood surrounded the pond and garden area. The fairy lights, which turned out to be candles in globe lanterns, failed to reveal the extent of the gardens or the type of plantings, and Estral decided she would have to explore the grounds in daylight. As they neared the pond, she saw that there were lanterns afloat in miniature boats. The scene, with the light reflecting on the still water, and fireflies blinking in the air, was enchanting and, dare she say, very Eletianlike.

On the far side of the pond they crossed a bridge over a stream that flowed from a grotto of moss and fern. Estral smiled at the musical drip and splash of water. Beyond the grotto was the folly, the tower she'd seen from the distance, its heights invisible in the dark of night. At its base, however, torches flared on either side of the entrance, ironbound doors standing wide open in welcome.

"I cannot remember the last time we had a party out here," Miss Bunch said. "Can you, Bay?"

"Heavens, no, but mother used to host teas and galas frequently. Do you recall?"

"Oh, yes. Father used to get so testy because they distracted him from his great work."

Professor Berry, Estral knew, had studied the arcane arts. With Sacoridia so phobic of magic, he'd been cast out of Selium for pursuing so dangerous and forbidden a field. That had been well before her own father's time as Golden Guardian, and she thought that, nowadays, someone with that kind of knowledge would be an inestimable resource when it came to understanding the increase in magic in the land after it had lain dormant for so long, and so much about it was forgotten.

Lamps and lanterns and candles illuminated the circular space of the tower interior. Just within reach of the light, grotesque faces in stone glared down at them. Estral could discern no ceiling for the chamber above the faces was obscured in shadow. A long table practically bowed beneath the burden of food, enough for a sumptuous feast for dozens of people. Platters were heaped with roasted meats, and there were bowls and dishes of salted potatoes, fiddleheads and leeks slathered in butter, cheese pies and pickled beets, and mashed turnips. There were muffins and breads and soups, and for dessert, numerous pies and cakes and tarts. Stickles was already bent over sniffing a roast pig. It was much too much, she thought, for four people.

"Where are all the guests?" she asked Miss Bunch.

"Why, right here in the tower."

Trying to say it as politely as she could, Estral said, "There are only four of us."

"The others are here." Miss Bay raised the lantern to eye level. "Or soon to be here with the light of the draugmkelder."

"*Draugmkelder.*" The word flowed unfamiliarly off Estral's tongue. It did not sound like Old Sacoridian or any other language she had encountered. "What is a draugmkelder, and what does it have to do with party guests?"

"It's a dream gatherer," Miss Bunch said.

Well, *that* explained everything. "I'm afraid I don't understand." She followed the sisters over to a wall hook from which they hung it. Miss Bay opened one of the tin panels to access the wick while Miss Bunch retrieved a candle from a sconce with which to light it.

"It gathers dreams from sleepers, most usually from people you know, which is most enjoyable. And through the dreams we can draw the dreamers to us and visit with them no matter how far-flung they may be."

"Father once tried to explain it to us," Miss Bay said. "He told us it creates a thinning between the realms of sleep and waking, but I'm not sure he really knew how it works himself."

At first Estral could only stare, but the sisters did not tell her they were having a joke on her, or that it was just a legend. No, by their demeanors she could tell they were utterly serious. She took a breath and tried to remind herself she'd seen and heard some pretty strange things herself. How much stranger could a draugmkelder be?

When she collected herself, she asked, "Do we have to be asleep for it to work?"

Miss Bunch applied the candle flame to the lantern's wick. "Now how could we light the lantern if we were asleep? Or enjoy any of Letitia's delicious cooking?" The flame seemed to die for a moment, but then it flared. When she removed the candle, the lantern glowed. Instead of giving off an oily scent, however, it smelled of an exotic spice or herb.

"What is that scent?" she asked. "I can't place it."

"Pleasant, is it not?" Miss Bay replied. "A little like sandalwood, but not. We are not sure what it is. The draugmkelder comes from far away. Father traced it as far as the Hasjii people of the great sands of the desert lands. The Hasjii are far-ranging traders. But the lantern itself probably came across an ocean or two before it arrived into Hasjii hands."

The lantern continued to glow brighter, and when Miss Bunch closed its door, it cast constellations against the wall, constellations Estral did not recognize, but must depict the sky from wherever the draugmkelder had originated. As for the Hasjii traders, she'd heard something of them, but even the Fioris did not travel deeply into the desert lands.

"What happens now?" she asked.

"We await the dreamers," Miss Bay replied, and she settled herself into a cushioned chair. "Could take a while."

Estral still struggled with the whole concept. The party guests were to be *dreamers* drawn to—through?—the draugmkelder from who-knew-where by their *dreams*.

Miss Bunch eased into another chair near her sister. Estral was too restless to sit around and wait for the "guests" to arrive. "I'd like to climb to the top of the tower, but I see no stairs."

The sisters chuckled.

"There are none, dear child," Miss Bunch said. "The tower is a *folly* after all. There are no steps and no upper floors. It is quite hollow. Our father used to call it his sorcerer's tower, and when mother was not holding one of her galas, he would come out here to sit and think."

"Or stand by the pond to throw stones into the water," Miss Bay said, "as males are wont to do."

"Help yourself to wine and food," Miss Bunch said. "Letitia has outdone herself. The festivities will commence eventually."

Estral glanced at the table. Stickles was shoving a meat-roll down his gullet. Not feeling particularly hungry herself, she glanced once more at the light of the draugmkelder playing against the wall, and then left the tower and found a rock to sit on next to the pond and listened to the very ordinary spring chorusing of frogs.

How long would it be before dreamers started appearing? She was not sure she wanted to see into someone else's dreams.

She was intrigued by the notion, but it also struck her as intrusive. Dreams were private affairs, the innermost visions of one's unconscious mind. Many felt dreams were filled with symbolism that reflected the dreamer's state of being in waking life. Did she or anyone else have the right to breach so private a domain?

In any case, it was apt to take a while, though time at Seven Chimneys was . . . odd. She picked up a pebble, weighed it in her hand, and considered. It felt as if she'd been the guest of the sisters for days, not just an afternoon. It was like being caught in the haze of a long-running dream where time did not obey the usual rules, but slowed down or sped up according to the needs of those who dwelled there. It must just be, she decided, another eccentricity of the place.

She shrugged and tossed the pebble into the pond breaking the still surface. It wasn't just males, she thought, who liked throwing rocks into water. The reflected light of floating lanterns wrinkled with the ripples her pebble produced. She yawned and was casting about for another pebble when a luminous blue-gray haze materialized in the air before her.

Dreamer

Estral sat up with a start thinking she'd fallen asleep and was dreaming, but she felt awake enough. She pinched herself to make sure.

"*Ow!*" Yes, definitely awake.

She watched in amazement as the luminous cloud that was floating before her disgorged dozens of fluffy winged kittens that took to the air as if it were the most natural thing in the world. It had to be the work of the draugmkelder. She laughed in delight at the aerobatics of the kittens as they fly-pounced on one another or chased their tails, and meeped and meowed as they played. A couple batted at real fireflies and she wondered how dream creatures could interact with the waking world like that.

It must be through the mind's eye of the dreamer, she thought, but of course she didn't really know. She was pretty certain, however, she knew *who* the dreamer was. But what did she do now besides enjoy the antics of the kittens?

"Call to him, child."

Estral almost fell off her rock, so startled was she by Miss Bay's sudden appearance at her side.

Call to him? And then what?

"Call to him," Miss Bay said again, "and he will join us, or he will not." She stuck her cane out so a kitten could perch on it. Her usually stern expression was broken with a smile of delight.

The kitten then leaped into the air to chase after its siblings, and Miss Bay slowly made her way back toward the tower.

So, Estral just had to call to the dreamer and he would appear. Or, he would not. She cleared her throat, and feeling a little self-conscious, called, "Alton! Alton, are you there?"

The kittens flew in a gyre until they were no more than a blurred vortex that turned, once more, into a drifting haze.

A little disappointed, she tried again. "Alton! It's me, Estral!"

Nothing happened except that the haze dissipated. Her disappointment grew for she had not seen Alton, her lover, since early winter when she'd slipped away from the encampment at the D'Yer Wall without telling him. She'd taken the coward's way out and left him a note informing him of her plan to travel north in search of her father. It had been a terrible thing to do, leaving like that, *selfish,* but she knew he would have tried to stop her, which would have led to arguments and much unpleasantness. And, worst of all, the temptation to stay put.

She called out again, but to no avail. She waited and waited, but just when she was ready to give up, a transparent figure came stumbling out of the dark along the edge of the pond. Barefoot and hair tousled, and wearing only a nightshirt, he looked disoriented.

Estral leaped to her feet. *"Alton?"*

"Where did the kittens go?" he asked. "I've got to follow the kittens because of the test."

"What test?"

"Mathematics." His voice was like a tired sigh. "I keep

having to take this test even though I'm no longer in school. Need to find the kittens . . . "

"The kittens have left," she replied.

He came to an ungainly halt in front of her. "Where have they gone? I've got to take the test."

He was still caught in a dream state, she thought. "Are you really here?" She reached out to touch his face and her hand passed through it, and yet . . . it did not. She could almost feel the warmth of his skin and the scruff of beard on his chin, but could not firmly touch him.

He mimicked her and tried to touch her face, but his hand passed through her. "I'd better go take that test."

"Alton," she said, "don't go. This is more than a dream—you're at the estate of the Berry sisters. Do you remember Karigan talking about them? They're having a party. You are here through your dreaming. *You are really here!*"

"This is another dream and you are a ghost."

"No! You are really here with me at Seven Chimneys. I mean, sort of." She'd missed him so much and truly wished for him to be there with her. She reached for his arm, felt that warmth again, and instinctively *pulled* with both her hands and her mind. He stumbled into her and shed translucence like a vaporous cloak. He turned completely solid in her arms.

"I *am* dreaming, aren't I?" he asked in a groggy voice.

She placed her hands on either side of his face and kissed him soundly.

Afterward, sounding a little more awake, he said, "If this is a dream, I like it. Feels real."

She kissed him again to convince him. She had to steady him when they at last parted.

"How is this possible?" he asked. "I was asleep in my cot,

103

dreaming . . . " He glanced about wide-eyed, and scratched his head. "Now I can't remember."

"You were looking for flying kittens because you had a mathematics test."

He frowned. "I dream about that test all the time, but the kitten part is new. Guess it's because Midnight has begun to nest."

"That is wonderful news!" It had been hoped that the gryphon pair—Midnight and Mister Whiskers—would produce offspring to help protect the D'Yer Wall from incursions by denizens of Blackveil Forest. She flung her arms around him and they hugged for a long time. "How I've missed you!"

"Me, too." When they parted, he said, "Explain this all to me, what I'm doing here, what this place is." His expression was one of awe as he took in the lights bobbing on the pond, and the tower looming behind them.

"I can't say as I understand everything myself, but I'll try to explain."

They strolled the paths around the pond hand-in-hand as she told him how she had arrived at Seven Chimneys, and about the sisters' draugmkelder. When that all sank in, he questioned her about her adventures in the north as he'd heard only sketchy details. She did not know how many circuits they made of the pond, but when she finished with her father's death, he just held her. She did not cry but found comfort with him right there, something she'd yearned for, for so long, her face pressed against the warmth of his shoulder. The magic of the draugmkelder was truly a gift.

"How long do we have?" Alton asked. "I mean, I assume I'll get sent back at some point." Then he looked down at himself. "Glad I decided to wear something to bed." They laughed.

104

"I don't know how it works," she told him, "how you go back or when. Or if. The sisters have been quite vague on the particulars."

"Maybe I'll have to go to Selium with you," he said.

She would love nothing more than to have him by her side as official mourning for her father began and she assumed the title and duties of the Golden Guardian. There would be ceremonies and eulogies, and important people from all around Sacoridia and other lands who would gather to bring her their condolences, and to stand witness to her investiture. It would be overwhelming, but his presence would make it bearable.

He leaned toward her and said, "I'd like to meet the Berry sisters. Karigan told me about them, but I don't think I ever quite believed all she said."

"This way." She took his hand once more. "When you see them, you'll believe."

She led him into the tower and was surprised to find it full of people and noisy with conversation and laughter. All the guests appeared to be in some form of night dress, though one portly gentleman had borrowed the table cloth to drape about himself. A few figures were hazy and transparent as Alton had been when he first arrived. Children chased after someone's dream of dragonlike lizards that spouted tiny flames as they leaped and flew through the crowd. One transparent figure glided above on air currents, arms spread wide in flight. Estral spotted Stickles, who was sure and solid and undeterred by the commotion around him. He had not left the table and currently gripped a drumstick in one fist and a wedge of pie in the other.

"There they are." Estral pointed to where the sisters presided over the affair like enthroned queens, guests clustering around them as supplicants. The guests parted to let Estral and Alton through. When Miss Bay finished speaking to a distinguished man in opulent silks, Estral said, "Miss Bay, Miss Bunch, this is—"

"Oh, don't tell us!" Miss Bunch said, nearly bouncing in her seat.

"It is obvious," Miss Bay told her.

"It is? No, no, let me guess." Miss Bunch peered hard at Alton. "A striking young man, isn't he. I don't think he's a pirate."

"Of course he's not a pirate. Look at his hands."

Alton raised his hands so Miss Bunch could examine them.

"Why, yes. Someone who works with his hands. A blacksmith, or maybe a stonecutter. But the Golden Guardian would not be with a blacksmith, would she. It would not be appropriate."

"It wouldn't?" Estral asked.

"Child, you are the Golden Guardian. You would need someone of like station to court you, so therefore he is a D'Yer. The D'Yers are stoneworkers and the lords of D'Yer Province. So I say this is Lord Quelvan D'Yer."

"Quelvan?" Estral asked, as surprised as Alton looked.

"Did I guess wrong?" said Miss Bunch. "Are you actually a blacksmith, young man?"

"Er, Quelvan was my great great grandfather," he replied. "I'm Alton." And he bowed.

"Oh, my, it appears we're a little behind the times," Miss Bunch said. Her sister just looked appalled. "But I did get the family right."

Miss Bay squinted and leaned toward Alton. "I believe the boy is more than just a lordling who can cut stone, sister."

"Oh?"

"Indeed. I would wager my eye tooth that this one is a Green Rider."

"I do not want your eye tooth, Bay." Miss Bunch's face wrinkled in disgust. "So it is not necessary to offer wagers. And I concur. Are you a Green Rider, young man?"

"I am," he said. "How did you guess?"

"We've known enough Green Riders to have the scent of them, so to speak," Miss Bay replied, "even though your arcane object did not travel with you."

"My arcane . . . ?"

"I think she means your brooch," Estral said. Green Riders wore winged horse brooches that, like Estral's harp brooch, were their badge of office, but also augmented minor special abilities in magic that otherwise lay dormant. Alton's ability was to put up an invisible shield of protection in times of danger.

He placed his hand on his chest where his brooch was usually clasped. "How do you know about . . . ?"

"We are quite aware of them," Miss Bay said, her eyes hooded.

Few knew the brooches existed for a spell of concealment lay upon them. They were supposed to have been destroyed centuries ago by those who distrusted magic, but the Riders of that time had managed to hide them instead, thus preserving their special abilities. The Green Riders remained secretive about their magic for their personal safety, and because they were king's messengers. If the populace knew the king relied on magic users to bear his messages, there would be outrage and upheaval, which would be bad enough during times of peace, but would be worse during times of strife, as now, when they were dealing with aggression from Second

Empire and needed a united front. Estral could only guess the sisters knew of them from their father's work, or perhaps one of the Riders they had known had confided in them.

"But . . . " Alton did not seem to know what to make of the fact that the sisters knew about Rider brooches.

Estral poked him in the ribs. "You aren't going to get any answers out of them," she whispered. "Believe me. I've tried."

"Are you enjoying the party?" Miss Bunch asked.

"What?" The change of topic threw him, which undoubtedly Miss Bunch intended. He swallowed hard, cleared his throat. "Oh, right, the party. It's—it's amazing."

The noise had not abated. There was much laughter and the clinking of wine glasses. Butterflies—no, fairies with butterfly wings—erupted from the mouth of a transparent dream man.

"Who are all these people?" Estral asked.

"Some distant relations," Miss Bay said, "and old friends, like Prince Dakher over there." She pointed to the gentleman in the fine silks they'd seen speaking with the sisters earlier.

"You mean the king of Tallitre?" Alton said in astonishment.

"Is he king now?" Miss Bay asked.

"I did say we were behind the times," Miss Bunch replied.

Her sister ignored her and pointed toward a big bearded dream man smoking a pipe with a meditative expression on his face. Mushrooms sprouted at his feet and a barred owl perched on his shoulder. "And there's that forester who takes care of the king's woods this side of the village of North."

"There are a few random strangers, too," Miss Bunch said with a shrug.

"When does it all end?" Estral asked, anxious to have as much time with Alton as possible. "And how?"

"When the draugmkelder extinguishes itself," Miss Bay said, "the dreamers will return to from wherever they've come."

"Will we remember any of this?" Alton asked.

"It will be like a dream. Some will remember something of its essence, and for others it will just slip away, lost to memory as dreams often are."

Estral and Alton moved off so the sisters could speak with more of their guests.

"Strangest party I've ever been to," he said.

"Same here."

"Estral . . . " He paused, looked down at the ground.

"Yes?"

When he gazed back up at her, his eyes were intense. "I don't want to forget our time together. I don't want you to slip away."

The Nightmare

"I won't slip away," Estral told Alton. "Not ever. And I'll be sure to remind you about all of this later so you know it wasn't just a dream."

"Good, because I love you and I don't want to forget being here with you. And I don't want to forget the Berry sisters, either. Those old girls are something else. Karigan was not exaggerating when she talked about them. In fact, she may have understated their . . . their . . ."

"Eccentricities?"

"Yes, that's it." Then he whispered, "They know about the brooches."

She whispered back, "Yes, they do," and patted his arm. They departed the tower for the shore of the pond where it was quieter.

"You should come back to the wall so we can be together," he said. "Your voice is working—it sounds so strong. You could sing for the guardians, help mend the wall."

"My place is in Selium right now. Besides, my voice is temporary, some magic of Seven Chimneys."

"I'm sorry," he said. "To have your voice and then have it taken away again must be hard."

"I am grateful to have it, for however short a time, to be able to talk with you rather than having to constantly scribble on my slate to say something."

110

"And it was really dense of me to ask you to come to the wall. Of course you can't. You are needed in Selium."

"*You* could come to Selium."

"I'll try," he replied, "but my orders are to stay at the wall."

Alton's ancestors had built the D'Yer Wall which protected Sacoridia from evil forces within Blackveil Forest. He was the one person in his clan who could communicate with the ghostly guardians in the wall. But as a king's messenger, he must also obey orders.

Estral opened her mouth to reply, but a movement, black against black near the pond's edge, caught her attention. She squinted, decided she was imagining things, and was about to turn back to Alton, but paused when she detected more movement.

"What is it?" he asked.

"I don't know. Nothing or maybe someone's dream. Which sounds strange to say aloud."

"True enough."

There was the movement again, this time closer. Lanterns flickered as if someone or something moved in front of them. She had the impression of a treelike figure, limbs blowing in a maelstrom. Then it came roaring at them and reared over them, massive and oozing malevolence. They fell back.

"What the hells?" Alton shouted.

It was a great black shadow vaguely human in shape, and it carried in its fist a whip. Several knotted thongs hung from its handle.

"No," Estral murmured. "No . . . "

"What is it?" Alton asked.

The creature raised the whip. Shadow blood dripped from the thongs.

"Run!" Estral cried.

Alton did not hesitate and they made for the tower. Estral could almost feel the shadow's black breath on the back of her neck. The whistling of the whip through the air was a sound with which she was all too familiar. It lashed the ground at their heels.

Estral and Alton waved their arms and shouted at party guests who'd wandered outside to run for cover. It took most of them a moment or two to understand. When they saw the shadow and the warning finally sank in, they bolted for the tower, Estral and Alton right behind them.

"The doors!" Alton yelled as they crossed the threshold. "Close and bar the doors!"

A number of guests, picking up on his urgency, heaved to, closing the heavy doors and barring them. A scream of rage from the thwarted shadow creature, now locked outside, curdled Estral's blood. There was a thud and the doors rattled. Guests cried out, their faces anxious in the lamplight, but most did not know what was going on.

The Berry sisters made their way through the crowd to Estral and Alton.

"What is all this ruckus?" Miss Bay demanded. "It is disrupting the party."

"A shadow creature!" Estral said, and she and Alton took turns describing what had happened. When they finished, the sisters gazed hard at one another. The shadow continued to bang on the doors and cry out its rage. Many of the guests cowered toward the far side of the tower.

"I told you what could happen," Miss Bunch said to her sister.

"I told *you*."

"You did not. *I* was the one who warned *you* about—"

Estral held her hands up to forestall a full-fledged sisterly quarrel. She wondered how long the door would hold up to the beating. "What were you afraid of happening? What is that thing out there?"

The sisters exchanged glances, and finally Miss Bunch answered, "Sometimes bad things can come through the draugmkelder. Not all dreams are happy after all, and everyone has at least a little bit of darkness in them."

"So this creature is a—a *nightmare*?" Alton demanded.

An explosive *BOOM!* shuddered the doors as if to punctuate his question. The hinges appeared to weaken under the assault and creaked against the timbers that framed the doors.

"In a word," Miss Bay replied, "yes. A 'nightmare' is a most apt descriptor."

"Well, if it gets in here, it's going to do some real damage and maybe hurt people. Er, can it hurt those of us who dreamed our way here?"

"Yes," Miss Bunch said. "Those of you who are corporeal in your presence like yourself, as well as non-dreamers like Lady Fiori and ourselves may be harmed. Dear, oh dear, what have we done?"

Estral thought fast. "The draugmkelder is a lantern, right? Couldn't we just extinguish its light to break the spell?"

"We could," Miss Bay said, "buuuut—"

"There would be consequences," Miss Bunch finished. "One thing our father learned over the years is that magic is rarely convenient."

BOOM!

Estral's nerves jangled with each pound on the doors. She reached for Alton's hand and clasped it firmly. He gave her a gentle squeeze in return and smiled. It calmed her.

"Extinguishing the draugmkelder," Miss Bunch continued, "could do unknown harm to the dreamers—permanently hurt their minds or perhaps even kill them. It needs to burn out on its own."

Estral wanted to shake the sisters and demand what they thought they were doing using such a dangerous magical device for their entertainment, but then, if they hadn't, she wouldn't have gotten to see Alton. And of course, berating them wouldn't do anyone any good at the moment. She gripped Alton's hand hard and he looked at her in surprise. She would not let anything happen to him. She wouldn't.

BOOM!

Some of the guests were crying and holding onto one another. Wood splintered around the hinges. Alton let her go and stalked toward the doors. He paused as if sizing up the situation.

"Alton?" Estral called.

He raised his hands, palms outward, and she realized he was calling on his magical ability to shield. She held her breath hoping he'd succeed, but when the creature attacked the doors once more and wood continued to splinter, his hands dropped to his sides and he returned to them.

"My ability isn't working without my brooch," he said.

"That is most unfortunate," Miss Bunch said. Miss Bay nodded in agreement.

"Then what in five hells do we do?" he demanded. "Those doors aren't going to hold. Can we kill the shadow?"

"Killing it is possible, I believe," Miss Bunch said, "but you may damage the nightmare's dreamer."

"At this point, I don't care. We need to protect ourselves."

Miss Bunch licked her lips. "You may find that an unpalatable solution as the nightmare is being dreamed by someone you know, and I believe care for."

"Who?"

BOOM! Followed by a terrible *crrraaack* as a hinge finally gave way.

Estral looked up at Alton. "Karigan. The dreamer is Karigan."

"*Karigan* is dreaming that thing?"

"If you had been there and seen exactly what she went through—"

The banging stopped and the shadow cackled. The hair rose on the nape of Estral's neck.

"Quickly," she said to the sisters, "how do we fix this?"

"You must reach the dreamer," Miss Bay answered, "and persuade her to stop dreaming the nightmare, get her to wake up."

"Persuade . . . ? She's miles and miles from here, only the gods know where."

Alton wrapped his arm around her shoulders. "You got *me* here all the way from the wall. There's got to be a way to reach her."

But then the one door crashed down in a cloud of dust and Alton pulled her away. Everyone pressed toward the back wall. The shadow ducked under the lintel and stepped into the tower chamber. When it straightened to its full height, its figure struck Estral as female and familiar, which did not surprise her in the least. The person who had tortured Karigan, the whip-wielding Nyssa, had been a woman.

The creature snapped the whip overhead through insubstantial dream images floating above and shredded them. What was left disintegrated immediately. One—a woman—screamed in agony before it vanished.

"Karigan!" Estral cried, not sure how she was supposed to get through to her friend. "Karigan, wake up!" That was the usual way to dislodge a nightmare, wasn't it? To wake up?

The shadow hurled the whip against the table, and food and crockery exploded in all directions. Those hidden beneath the table scrambled and crawled away.

"Is there another way out?" Alton shouted at the sisters.

"No, child," Miss Bunch replied. "There is only the one entrance."

The tower was a folly in more than name, Estral thought.

The whip came down again on the table, and wire barbs knotted into the thongs left grooves in the wood.

Then, from the trembling mass against the far wall, one man sprinted across the floor to stand before the shadow. It was Stickles and he wielded a carving knife.

"No!" Estral cried, remembering what Miss Bunch had said about how harming the shadow could harm the dreamer. *Karigan.*

The shadow looked down on Stickles and hurled the whip at him. He jumped aside just in time, then rushed the creature and stabbed it in the leg. The shadow's howl of pain quaked the tower, showering dust down on them.

"Alton!" Estral said. "He's hurting Karigan when he stabs the shadow!"

"Wait here." Alton ran into the fray dodging the thrashing of the whip. Stickles raised the knife again, but before he could plunge it into the shadow, Alton grabbed his wrist and tackled him to the floor. The shadow looked down at the two men rolling between its feet. Stickles might seem to be all bones, but he was wiry strong and squirmed out of Alton's hold.

Alton staggered to his feet, wrenched Stickles's arm, and spun him around. He planted a sound fist in the pirate's face. Estral felt for Stickles, knowing the strength of those stone-cutter hands. Strong as the granite itself.

116

The knife clattered to the floor, and Stickles rolled away and curled into a fetal position and did not move. Alton, breathing hard, rubbed his hand as he watched after Stickles. The shadow loomed over him.

"Alton!" Estral cried, but she was too late.

Giving Voice

The shadow grabbed Alton around the neck and lifted him off his feet.

"No!" Estral cried.

Alton struggled, trying to pry away shadow fingers that squeezed his throat.

"Karigan!" Estral shouted in desperation. *"Wake up!"* Then as a whisper she added, "Oh, please wake up, your nightmare is hurting Alton."

But it was to no avail. The guests remained huddled together sobbing and clinging to one another as the shadow strangled the one she loved, choking the life out of him. She couldn't be responsible for failing him, too. She—

To her surprise, Miss Bay hobbled by her at a good clip bound for the shadow.

"Bay!" Miss Bunch cried out from Estral's side. "What are you doing?"

"The girl is feeling sorry for herself again and being quite useless, so someone has got to do something."

Estral's mouth fell open as Miss Bay went right up to the shadow and walloped it with her cane. The shadow made a questioning sound and gazed down at her.

"Filthy beast!" Miss Bay chided it. "You are ruining our party. Put the young man down immediately."

When the shadow did not comply, she whacked it with

her cane once more, and kept whacking until it sidled away. She followed and must have hit a sensitive spot because it roared and dropped Alton. He fell to his hands and knees and started retching. Estral was about to run to him when Miss Bunch grabbed her arm.

"You must help! You must reach Bay or—"

The shadow growled at Miss Bay. It fingered the tendrils of its whip as if thinking about what vengeance it could wreak upon the irritating woman.

"Remember the benevolence of the house," Miss Bunch said. *"Use your voice."*

But Estral had been using her voice to yell at Karigan to wake up, hadn't she? What else could she do? How else could she—?

"Bay!" Miss Bunch cried. "You leave that shadow at once and come back here."

Miss Bay, who was apparently in no mood to listen to her sister, raised her cane to lay another one on the shadow. Alton climbed to his feet and moved toward her. The shadow gathered its whip and cast it back in order to deal its irritant a mighty blow.

They were both in danger—Alton and Miss Bay, even as he attempted to take her arm to lead her away. They would not be fast enough. Estral had to act. She was not like Karigan who rushed into danger with sword drawn, but she possessed her own strengths. *Use your voice,* Miss Bunch had said. Her words finally sank in and Estral knew what she had to do. She drew in a deep breath, felt the expansion of her diaphragm, felt song rise from every part of her, from her toes to her crown. It flowed through her throat, filled her mouth. Her whole being vibrated. She was song.

After Karigan's torture, while she'd lain hurt and bleeding,

Estral had sung songs of healing as taught to her by their Eletian guide, Enver. It may have helped Karigan rest, may have helped her heal, but she did not know for sure. Now, however, she'd never felt song so visceral. It awakened her to the very roots of her hair and tingled. Maybe it was the benevolence of the house boosting her strength, giving her a voice, but it was in fact truly hers, and as she released the song, she felt as if she were soaring. The tall hollow tower amplified the sound and enveloped everyone in resonance until they, too, became song.

It was song without words, harmony taking flight. Estral could not reverse the harm that had been done to Karigan, the result of her own misguided actions, but she could at least try to provide her friend comfort, a respite from the nightmare that tortured her. She gave it everything, all her vocal power and skill, and all her heart, for the friend she loved who had suffered more than anyone should.

It was a song of healing, a song of redemption. It unlocked her prison of grief and guilt and self-loathing, and so she was able to spare a little love for herself, too.

A glance when she paused for another breath revealed Alton bringing Miss Bay to the arms of her sister. Stickles was nowhere to be seen. The shadow stood frozen, its gaze locked on her. She sensed more than saw the burning eyes and anger, the joy it felt in mutilating others. A moment of fear passed through her as chill and sharp as a dagger because this was no ordinary nightmare. It was very *present* as if the torturer it represented still held power even though she was dead. Estral could not imagine the torment Karigan still experienced under its influence.

The shadow stepped forward. Fear washed over Estral anew and she wavered, but then Alton was there beside her.

"You are amazing," he told her. "You can do this. I'll stand with you, no matter what."

She sang again as the shadow advanced, her voice quavering at first, but strengthening with melodies of streams and meadows and mountains, of gentle rainfall on a roof, of spring leaves fluttering in a breeze. It filled everyone in the tower with peace, she knew, just as it filled her.

The fire of the shadow's eyes cooled. The thongs of the whip trailed along the floor, limp with no muscle to wield it. The creature shrank and shrank and yet doggedly staggered forward, so determined was it to be the nightmare.

Estral kept singing even as it came within arm's reach, but by now it was tiny, its roars a squeak, and of a sudden it erupted into a puff of vapor that drifted away on a breeze. No anger, no turmoil, no cruelty remained. Instead, a transparent figure wrapped in blankets lay just outside the broken doorway with a green greatcoat folded as a pillow beneath her head.

"Karigan," Alton whispered.

Estral brought the song down to a soft final note and let the air currents carry the last of it away. The spell held for but a moment before the party guests started moving and chatting as if awakening from a long nap.

Estral and Alton, followed by the Berry sisters, approached Karigan's sleeping form on tip-toes. They did not wish to disturb her. Her dream presence was one of serenity and deep sleep, very much in contrast to what she must have experienced during the nightmare.

"Are you going to bring her all the way here like you did me?" Alton asked. "She does not look . . . well."

Estral gazed at her friend's pale face, still much too thin

from all she'd endured in the north. Ragged, shorn hair brushed across hollow cheeks. She lay on her stomach, which meant her back still pained her too much to sleep on it.

"No," she replied.

Alton nodded. Estral could not guess what was going through his mind—Karigan looked so unguarded, so vulnerable. The two had been almost-lovers, a relationship that had been complicated by their busy lives as Green Riders and a reluctance on Karigan's part. He'd been aghast and horrified as Estral had told him about the torture as they walked around the pond earlier. Perhaps now, seeing Karigan like this, so transformed from when last he'd seen her, made her story truly sink in. His expression was tender as he gazed down at Karigan.

"I wonder if I ever really knew her," he murmured. "All that she has done, all that she has been through . . . "

"It is wise to let her rest undisturbed," Miss Bay said. "It is a rare gift for one who has been so troubled."

"Sing her away," Miss Bunch told Estral, "to ensure her peaceful sleep continues."

This time when Estral sang, it was not the soaring vocals of before, but a gentle softer tune, a lullaby of sorts. The dream image of Karigan wavered and then faded away.

"Well done," Miss Bunch said. "You've undoubtedly helped your friend more than you know. Your singing will not keep the nightmares away permanently, but what you did tonight cannot be underestimated for the relief the peace will bring." She squeezed Estral's shoulder, and then she and Miss Bay walked away to attend to their other guests.

Estral closed her eyes and exhaled, wishing to retain the sense of serenity she'd conjured with the singing. Her guilt over what had been done to Karigan, and the part she believed she played in her father's death, would always be there, but now she felt some sense of atonement. She'd been able to *help* her friend this time, and after seeing the manifestation of Karigan's nightmare, she knew it would make a difference. Providing help was a gift for Estral as much as for its recipient.

Alton placed his arm around her shoulders and she came back to herself.

"You all right?" he asked. "You must be exhausted."

"I'm fine," she replied. "In fact, better than fine. But maybe a little hungry. Shall we see if any food survived the rampage of the shadow?"

Alton smiled and was about to respond when Stickles ran back into the tower and almost barreled right into Estral.

"You've gotta come!" He grabbed her arm and shook it.

"I've got to come *where?*" Estral asked, observing that his eye was almost swollen shut from Alton's punch.

"Follow me—you gotta help!"

She and Alton exchanged glances and followed when Stickles sprinted from the tower. She could not imagine what had excited the fellow so.

The Ocean on the Other Side
of the Pond

Drawn by Stickles's sense of urgency, Estral and Alton ran
after him all the way from the tower to the front of the house
where the bow of the ship loomed. When they stumbled to a
halt, they fought to catch their breath. Stickles was quick.

"This is going to be the most exhausting dream ever,"
Alton said when he finally could breathe again. Then he
gazed up at the silhouette of the bow against the stars in awe.
"You told me about this, but seeing it?"

"It's amazing, isn't it?" Estral said.

"Aye, it's a ship in a house." Stickles gave a dismissive
wave of his hand. "And we need the lady's help."

"We?" Estral asked.

Stickles pointed up at the figurehead. "Ceylene."

"It has a name?"

"*She. She* has a name. She's one of the merfolk and she
needs your help."

"One of the mer . . . " Alton began in disbelief.

"We sailors know them deep in the southern seas," Stickles said. "They are tricksters that lure unwary crews off
course with their beauty and song to break ships upon a
rocky ledge, or they'll cause a storm and rough seas, or . . . "

"Or lure you overboard to drown you," Alton interrupted.
"I've heard those stories before."

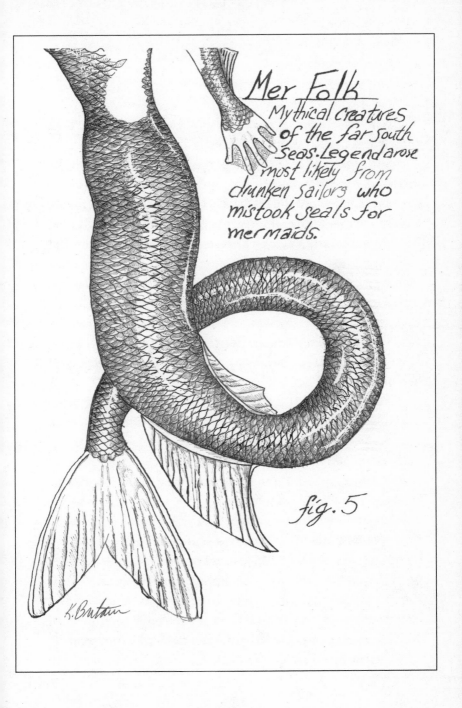

Mer Folk

Mythical creatures of the far south seas. Legend arose most likely from drunken sailors who mistook seals for mermaids.

fig. 5

K. Britain

So had Estral. In fact, she knew quite a few sea chanteys and legends about merfolk.

"Not stories, and they don't always drown us."

"Oh, really?"

"No, not always. If they take a liking to a man, he'll be spared as a mate. Become a merman."

"She's made of wood," Estral broke in. "Very beautifully rendered, but still wood."

"Aye, she's wood, but she wasn't always. The first captain who sailed this ship, many years before I came aboard, bound her to it with dark magic as a warning to the merfolk of what could happen to them if they caused his crew any mischief. Plus, he was pleased by his catch and wanted to show her off for all to see. It is said he believed her to be good luck."

"You are saying she was once a living being?"

"Still is, and long has she been trapped in this form. Y'see, I can sometimes hear her. Hear her sing, hear her weep, hear her speak to me."

It occurred to Estral that if Deckhand Stickles were hearing things, he might very well be mad. The whole situation *was* mad—the Berry sisters, the draugmkelder, dreams become real and nightmares going on rampages. After all this, how outrageous was it that there might be more to a figurehead than finely carved wood?

She gazed once more at the figurehead though it was hard to see in the night. Ship owners often placed figureheads on the prows of ships for luck, just as Stickles had said, but they were also an easy way for illiterate seamen to identify various ships. Some of the ship owners commissioned sculptures of immense beauty and artistic merit to show off their wealth, which was not, coincidentally, the best way to avoid pirates.

Figureheads *did* have an uncanny aspect, she thought, the

way they perpetually gazed out to sea unflinching whether in the midst of stormy conditions or calm, no matter if the figurehead was a lady in a fine gown, a warrior with sword drawn, or some mythical creature. They could be bawdy, romantic, or courageous, but always the resolute face of the ship. They did seem alive, in a way, dancing above the waves and always looking forward, so it was no surprise sailors projected superstitions on them, like luck.

"Your singing," Stickles said, "it started to wake her up—I know it did."

"How—?" She stopped herself. She'd been about to ask how her singing could possibly do such a thing, but this was Seven Chimneys and just this night she'd destroyed a nightmare with her voice.

Stickles visibly struggled with his patience. "I can *hear* her. You must sing more—it will free her. I know it will."

"Are you believing this?" Alton asked her.

"Do I believe *any* of this?" She spread her hands wide to indicate all of Seven Chimneys. "It can't hurt to try. Besides, you are one to ask, you with your gryphons."

He conceded the point with a nod.

Stickles was practically jumping up and down in agitation. "Place your hands on the hull—that'll help, and she'll feel your song even more."

"All right, all right," Estral muttered. She stepped up to the hull and found a space free of sharp barnacles. The wood was rough under her hands. She traced long narrow cavities where worms had chewed on it. Even outside, the scent of brine was strong, and when she closed her eyes, she could easily imagine herself by the sea, hear the calls of gulls, feel the undulation of waves. She considered singing a chantey, but discarded the idea not knowing if merfolk appreciated the songs of sailors. She decided to let the sea itself be her guide, thinking merfolk would be receptive to something more natural, more primal.

Her song conjured images of blue-green water breaking on the shore, of guillemots and cormorants floating with the currents. She visited seals sunning themselves on a rock ledge and followed them as they plunged into the depths in search of fish, into kelp forests, into the watery dark.

Soon her song was answered by another who knew the sea intimately and Estral shivered with the cold of the water and the alien quality of the voice. She flowed with the song's currents and found threads of sorrow and loneliness. Estral tried to extend comfort and friendship in her descant.

Of a sudden, the answering song grew dominant, turned into a scream in Estral's mind that made all the images shatter.

Someone shook her. "Estral?"

She opened her eyes to find Alton hovering over her, and dew-laden grass soaking into her back.

"Are you all right?" he asked.

She put her hand to her temple. "What happened?" She must have fainted.

"Look!" He helped her to her feet and took her to where Stickles stood with his arms wide open.

"I'll catch you," he told the figurehead.

To Estral's astonishment, the figurehead's tail glistened in the starlight as though wet, and her hair blew free of her shoulders. Where once there was wood grain, there was now flesh. Her body rippled with life.

"I can't believe it," she whispered.

Ceylene the mermaid tried to push herself off the hull, but she was stuck. Then she paused, took a deep breath, and sounded such a note of distress that it was pitched nearly above the range of hearing and caused windows to crack. Then came a splintering like boards being torn apart and Ceylene fell free. Alton leaped to help Stickles catch her. This accomplished, Stickles, who supported her upper body, leaned close to her face as if to catch whispered words.

"What did you say?" he asked her.

"Water," the mermaid said. "I need to be in water."

Stickles adjusted her in his arms. "To the pond!" he cried.

Alton and Estral helped support her tail as they ran once again, but this time to the back side of the house and down the lawn. The mermaid's tail was heavy with muscle, and smelled of fish and seaweed and . . . sawdust. Her scales felt like that of any fish—slippery and rough at the same time. The brown and greenish scales covered her all the way to just below her breasts, but under closer inspection, her breasts appeared to be covered in clear iridescent scales, only giving that part of her the illusion of human flesh.

By the time they reached the pond, Estral thought her arms would fall out of their sockets. Stickles waded right in up to his waist, she and Alton splashing behind with the tail. Cold water seeped through Estral's trousers up to her knees. Her feet sank into the soft bottom.

"Gently," Stickles said.

They lowered Ceylene into the water where she floated like a dead fish, her hair splayed on the pond's surface. The little boat lights turned the scales, which Estral had seen as brown and green, into a dazzle of gold and emerald.

"Shouldn't she be in ocean water?" Alton asked. "I mean, merfolk aren't freshwater folk, are they?"

Stickles supported Ceylene's upper body in the water, his face shadowed as he gazed down at her. "They prefer salt water," he replied, "but will swim up freshwater estuaries to spawn."

"Is she going to be all right?" Estral asked.

"I dunno." A boat light drifted close enough to unmask his concerned expression. "Maybe if you sang?"

Before Estral could open her mouth, however, gill slits opened on Ceylene's neck and she lifted her tail and slapped it on the water, splashing all three of them. Estral pushed wet hair out of her eyes just in time to see Ceylene slip out of Stickles's arms and disappear beneath the surface of the pond. Boat lights rocked in her wake.

"I guess that's that," Alton said.

Estral placed her hand on his arm. In the distance they saw a large form briefly break the surface, then dive again. Ceylene continued porpoising in a widening pattern until finally she paused before Stickles, her head and shoulders bobbing above the surface.

"I am free!" she cried in an elated voice. It had a breathy quality that may have had something to do with her gills. She swam closer to Estral. "You are a sister in song and blessed with a special voice, a voice of power—use it well." Ceylene smiled. Her needle-sharp teeth were those of a deep-sea carnivore's, which, given her otherwise pleasant features, was a little off-putting.

To Alton she said, "It is not often we merfolk find reason to thank terrestrial males. During my imprisonment, for all those years, I could only feel anger and the desire for vengeance against your kind. And yet, you helped save me. I will, perhaps, not be so quick to judge in the future. I thank you."

Alton bowed in return.

Ceylene drifted to where Stickles remained hip-deep in water.

"Will you come home with me?" she asked him. "Become one among the merfolk and be part of our song?"

"Home? The southern sea is far away. This is just a little pond. How will you get there?"

"Home is not as far away as you may think."

The pond then transformed. It brightened, and as Estral gazed into it, she experienced the sensation of being submerged on the ocean floor and looking upward toward the surface where shafts of sunlight burst through blue-green water. Colorful corals grew on a reef, and the water was dense with different kinds of fish darting here and there or swimming in schools. Others skulked in the rocks and crannies of the reef. A sea turtle paddled near the surface, a silhouette with the sun bearing down on it.

"Will you come, Stickles?" Ceylene asked. "It is not far."

Stickles scratched his chin. Something tiny plopped into the water—the barnacle. He looked at Estral and Alton, and liquid light of a far distant ocean reflected on his face.

"What—what do I do?" he asked them.

"What do you want to do?" Estral said. "What does your heart tell you?"

He looked down, not at Ceylene, not at anything.

"You were kind to me, Stickles," Ceylene said, "when no others were. You were the only one who could hear me. For all those years, it was your presence, your caring, that kept me sane. You listened to me and talked to me. I would have given up but for you and turned entirely to wood. But it is your decision. Know that you'd be welcome among the merfolk."

He gazed now at the mermaid. "I won't drown if I go with you?"

"I would not let that happen."

A smile crossed his face. "I've never been a fish before."

She held her hand out to him. Light glistened on the webbing between her fingers. He waded in deeper to meet her and took her hand. They gazed at one another as if they were the only two beings in the world, and then without warning or farewell, they submerged into the colorful world of coral and reef and out of Estral's ken.

Abruptly a great cacophony of gulls started crying from the direction of the house. They flew over to the pond and one by one dove into the water, arrowing to the other side where the ocean lay. They were followed by a few shearwaters and terns and other seabirds, and then finally a stray gannet that threw itself at the water in the ungainly way of the species—all wing and splash—and dove and dove and dove until it reached the sun.

With a suddenness that made Estral sit hard on the muddy bank, the ocean vanished and once more was a dark, serene pond.

The Seven Chimneys Rose

"Well," Alton said, "that was something." He offered Estral a hand up.

"It certainly was."

When she gazed upon the pond, all was as it had been before, no hint of the ocean, no mermaid, no Stickles. Ordinary frogs chorused their spring song, and the little boats bearing their lanterns drifted upon the water's silken surface undisturbed.

"I'm a bit chilly," Alton said. "Shall we return to the tower?"

They were both soaked through, and Alton, after all, had only his nightshirt.

"Let's go."

The Berry sisters met them halfway there.

"My, but it is not warm enough for a swim," Miss Bunch said, taking in their soggy condition.

Estral and Alton took turns explaining.

"Well," Miss Bay said when they finished, "there goes our new handyman."

"Just when I was growing rather fond of him." Miss Bunch dabbed her eyes with a lacy handkerchief.

"I for one am glad the mermaid is gone," Miss Bay said. "I didn't like the way she stared at me."

"She wasn't staring at you."

"Indeed she was, ogling me with those baleful eyes of hers."

Estral cleared her throat. "We are wet and cold."

"Dear me," Miss Bunch said, "but we'd be terrible hostesses if we did not provide comfort for our guests."

"Come, we'll take you to the cottage," Miss Bay said, setting off in a new direction.

"Cottage?" Alton asked.

"Yes, where you may dry yourselves off and relax in one another's company. Unless you'd prefer to spend the rest of the night shivering while you play a long and involved game of Intrigue with us."

"The cottage sounds fine." His answer may have been a touch quick. Miss Bay smirked.

The cottage was situated away from everything else on the estate, in a clearing in the woods. Moonlight puddled on its whitewashed walls where trellises supported climbing roses. Clusters of ferns, still furled so early in the season, crowded against the foundation. Smoke drifted from a single chimney and gold lamplight shone in the window.

"Enjoy," Miss Bunch said. "The draugmkelder is still likely to burn at least till dawn."

Estral and Alton followed stepping stones to the front door and pushed it open. Inside, it was a one room affair with a small kitchen area, table and chairs, and a bed positioned to the far end. Food was laid out for them—cold meats, bread and cheese, and wine. The rhubarb pie looked especially fine. Robes were laid out on the bed for them, and so they attended to removing their wet garb and setting it by the fire to dry. Then, finding themselves famished, they availed themselves of the food. Afterward, each with a glass of wine, they sat before the fire in armchairs and toasted the Berry sisters.

They sat in silence for a time just enjoying one another's company, until Estral said, "I feel like I should be worrying about a thousand things and that I should be sad about my father, but I can't feel anything at the moment except content and happy because I am in this cozy place with you."

"From what I gather," Alton replied, "you've already been doing a lot of grieving and feeling guilt over things that were not necessarily yours to control. I sort of feel the same way about the wall—I haven't been able to fix it and it may be Sacoridia's undoing."

"You didn't break the wall."

"No, but my clan is responsible for its upkeep and we failed in that. But right now, I am happy just like you to be here, to have a moment's peace without all the pressure and worry. We've been through a lot—you, me, Karigan, the Green Riders—and I suspect there is more to come. Don't we deserve a respite before the storm? And without it, how are we to have the energy and the will to carry on the fight? After all, what is it we are fighting for? There will be enough grief and worry to come."

She gazed at him and watched the firelight play across his face. "You're right. I hadn't thought of it that way before. A chance to rest and regroup. You know, Karigan once called me a wise old mother, but I think tonight that title belongs to you."

He chuckled. "I think the wise old mothers are those sisters. Look at this haven they gave us tonight." He paused, then added thoughtfully, "A haven so long as no other nightmares come through the draugmkelder." He rose and took her hand and raised her to her feet. "In any case, I think it would be *wise* to take advantage of it."

"Oh?" she smiled. "In what way?"

"In the way that I'll think I had one of *those* dreams when I wake up alone in my cot at the wall."

"Let's make it memorable then," she said, "shall we?"

Morning came far too soon, for all that time at Seven Chimneys seemed, well, flexible, allowing Estral and Alton all the time they wanted and then some. Still, morning came, and it was with sorrow that he was not beside her when she woke up. The magic of the draugmkelder had finally broken.

Someone had brought her breakfast and laid it out on the table while she slept, filled a hip bath with hot water, and cleaned, dried, and pressed her clothes. She was going to miss Seven Chimneys.

When she stepped outside, she took a moment to breathe deeply of the fresh, clean air. In the distance lay the pond with no hint of the previous night's excitement. The tower, however, seemed to have a kink in it that had not been there before, evidence of the nightmare's power. She shook her head and headed for the main house where she found the Berry sisters in the garden standing beside the statue of Marin. They were inspecting green shoots tentatively venturing out of the soil.

"Good morning," she called.

"Yes, it *is* a good morning," Miss Bunch said.

Miss Bay scowled at the sky as if she wasn't sure. There were large fluffy clouds passing overhead.

"You are rested?" Miss Bunch asked.

Despite all that had happened during the night, including her pleasant time with Alton, she had to say she felt extremely rested. She nodded.

"Good. The party was a tremendous success despite the

fright and damage wrought by the nightmare. But all was not fear and doom. One must make room for gaiety and lightness—even Bay."

Miss Bay grunted. "So says she who won at Intrigue last night."

"And resoundingly!" Miss Bunch's smile was enormous. "In any case, someone awaits you on the front drive."

Estral hurried, thinking that by some miracle Alton had returned, or maybe he somehow hadn't left. Her step faltered, however, when she reached the front of the house and found that the "someone" wasn't even human. Coda stood on the drive, his hide and tack agleam. She walked up to him and petted his neck.

"How'd you get here, boy?"

He snuffled her sleeve.

"He came trotting up the drive this morning," Miss Bay said when the sisters caught up with her. "Farnham found him grazing on the lawn and gave him some grain and a good brushing while you slept."

Estral wondered about Coda just trotting up the drive of his own volition. It wasn't like he was as smart as a Green Rider horse, but she did not dwell on it. One had to expect the unexpected at Seven Chimneys.

"You will find the rest of your companions awaiting you if you follow the drive into the woods." Miss Bay pointed the way with her cane.

"But I don't want to go."

"I know, child," Miss Bunch replied. "We may take the occasional respite, but the world turns on. There are many who rely on you, including those you love such as Lord Alton and our Karigan. The sooner you return, the sooner you can be with them, yes?"

Estral nodded. They were right. To hide at Seven Chimneys might be an escape from her responsibilities and the darkness of the outer world, but there were wonderful things out there, too. She mounted Coda.

"Before you leave," Miss Bay said, "we have something for you."

"Rather," Miss Bunch said, "it's for your father, in his memory." She handed Estral two small pouches. "One contains bunchberry seeds and the other bayberry to be planted around his resting place. Your father was known for his travels in Sacoridia's wild places where bayberry and bunchberry proliferate. I think he'd approve. Perhaps they will also provide you with solace and remind you of us."

Estral accepted the gifts and stashed them carefully in one of her saddlebags.

"One more thing," Miss Bay said. She handed Estral a yellow rose. "The Seven Chimneys Rose, our mother's favorite, to adorn your father's coffin on his journey to Selium. It blooms most of the year except in deepest winter, and it will not shrivel soon, and in fact it may take a liking to life in Selium."

"We sprouted there ourselves," Miss Bunch said.

"Thank you," Estral replied, moved by their gifts. Tears threatened to spill down her cheeks.

"Go now, child," Miss Bunch said, "and know that we derived much pleasure from your visit and that you are always welcome to come see us again."

Estral knew she had to go now or it would be too hard. She reined Coda down the drive. A quick glance over her shoulder revealed the sisters standing in place watching after her. She rode over the bridge and down the path. She'd forgotten to ask how to find the North Road, but she'd a feeling she'd have no trouble this time.

Her feeling turned out to be correct. The path led directly to the road, and there waiting for her was Lieutenant Rennard and the honor guard.

After greetings, Rennard said, "We were worried when you vanished, but then some odd old ladies came and told us you were visiting with them and that you'd return to us shortly. I can't explain it, but they felt very . . . trustworthy, and they promised you were safe." He scratched his chin and looked in the distance as if second-guessing himself. "Now that I think of it, the whole encounter was a little off, but at the same time . . . ? It felt right." He shook his head as if to clear off a fog. "You are well?"

"Very," she replied, her voice now back to its usual hoarse quality.

She rode over to the field carriage and gazed at the oilskin-covered coffin. She took a deep breath. Grief would be with her for a long time, but it would not occupy every moment of her life. She placed the rose on top of the coffin and immediately it seemed to grow, sprouting new buds and leaves. She smiled. She was taking a little bit of Seven Chimneys' magic home with her.

She returned to the front of the honor guard to take her place next to Rennard. She nodded and Rennard gave the order to move on. When she looked, the path to Seven Chimneys had vanished. She tried not to be too sad about it for the Berry sisters had invited her to visit again, and when the time was right, she was sure she'd find the path, and Seven Chimneys, awaiting her.

Sisters

The sisters watched as Estral rode away down the drive and into the woods.

"It was a very good visit," Bunch said.

"She will be an excellent Golden Guardian," Bay replied, "though it will take her some time to realize it and grow into the role."

"She took care of that nightmare, but I fear it won't be the last one for our Karigan. At least she has had a reprieve. As for our party, I daresay we should have more."

"What?" Bay said, "And invite more nightmares in?"

"You must admit, Bay, it does add color to the event. The party was great fun."

"Even when it nearly destroyed the folly?"

"What can I say? We put on a *good* party."

Bay gave her sister an aggravated look.

"All of us need to forget the cares of the world now and then," Bunch said, "to enable us to have the strength to face trouble when we really need it. Even if it means a few cracks in the mortar, broken doors, and the top third of the tower leaning askew."

Bay muttered imprecations under her breath.

"What is that, Bay? I am not sure I heard you."

"Be glad you did not."

The two turned around to study the bow of the ship rising above them.

"I do not miss *her*," Bay said. "Her gaze always accusing me of all the misdeeds toward merfolk committed by two-legged humanity. Why blame *me*? It's not like I'd ever seen a real mermaid before."

"Perhaps it was your sour disposition of which she disapproved," Bunch replied, causing Bay to huff. "I thought she was rather beautiful, myself. The bow does not look quite right without her."

"Well, commission a new figurehead, then."

"I just might. I hope Stickles likes his new life as a fish."

"A *skinny* fish."

Bunch sighed. "True love. He gave up everything to be with her."

"Humph and hogwash," Bay said. "What did he have to give up? A job as handyman? Not a hard decision. I will admit there is one thing that pleases me more than anything out of this whole affair, and it has nothing to do with love."

"Oh? Something that pleases *you*, Bay? Do tell."

"Yes. Look there, on the roof. What do you see?"

"The masts, the chimneys, shingles. That is all."

"Exactly!"

"I do not understand. You are being obtuse, sister."

"I am not. Don't you see? The seagulls are gone."

"Oh," Bunch said, "we are back on that topic again, are we? Really, Bay, you must stop obsessing about birds."

And so, the argument continued as the two made their way back to the kitchen entrance to have it out over a pot of tea.

AFTERWORD

About the Stories

"Wishwind"

"Wishwind" has been twenty-nine years in the making. I began writing it the summer of 1989, which was my first season working as a ranger at Acadia National Park. Naturally, on days off, I headed out to enjoy all the park had to offer, including sitting on a slab of pink granite to watch the ocean dash against the shore. On one such occasion, I took out pen and paper and began drafting what is now "Wishwind." You will note that 1989 was a few years before *Green Rider* was a mote in my eye, which means there was no Green Rider character, no Long War, and no Sacor Clans in the early drafts of "Wishwind"—those came later. However, Marin the Gardener was present from the beginning, and later showed up in *Green Rider* as a "sea witch" or "goddess" represented as a statue in the garden of the Berry sisters. Little did I know as I was writing that first draft of "Wishwind" that it would actually become linked to a series of fantasy novels.

Initially "Wishwind" was more a meditation on nature than a plot-heavy story. Though I have since expanded the plot, much of the meditation remains. I suppose the emphasis on nature is not surprising as I was falling in love with Acadia during the writing of that first draft, and had arrived there after having worked in major metropolitan areas. I found the landscape of Maine and Acadia healing, and, really, that's what "Wishwind" is about.

"Linked, on the Lake of Souls"

This story first appeared in the *DAW 30th Anniversary: Fantasy* anthology back in 2002. But for a few minor changes, it is the same story. However, it recently came into play in the sixth Green Rider novel, *Firebrand*, in a scene in which Estral tells Karigan a story. Instead of making up an entirely new tale for her to tell, I drew on one that already existed. Doing so saved me a few brain cells. And so here it is in its entirety for those who might have wondered about it and missed it when it debuted in 2002.

My goal with this story was to write about characters who got into deeper and deeper trouble, and how they fought their way out of it. Ultimately, it became a story about friendship, which is fitting for Estral and Karigan and the situation in which they find themselves in *Firebrand*.

"Linked" also has its roots in Acadia, but not necessarily in the wistful beauty of nature as in "Wishwind," but rather in the terror that lurks beneath the surface. Acadia bounds several lakes and ponds upon which visitors can canoe or kayak. When gliding over the glassy surface, a glance downward into the water may reveal the submerged trunks of trees like pale, slender limbs just below, reaching, reaching . . .

The Dream Gatherer

My agent had suggested a number of times that I should write a novella set in the world of my Green Rider Series. Doing so became more pertinent with the 20th anniversary approaching. I wasn't sure what the story would be, but a night or two before I was due to fly to Toronto to be a guest of honor at Ad Astra, a long-established science fiction and fantasy convention, I started thinking about the Berry sisters and the shambles in which I had left their house after *The High King's Tomb.* As I drifted to sleep, I hoped I would remember my thoughts so I could write them down later. Turns out I did remember, and I wrote the opening paragraphs as the airplane soared through the sky, the world lost to the clouds.

Because the novella was being written in honor of the anniversary of *Green Rider,* a visit with the Berry sisters seemed appropriate. After all, they debuted in the novel and proved memorable for many readers. And, also because of the anniversary, I wanted to make the story a celebration of sorts, hence the party the sisters throw, which, of course, goes awry.

ACKNOWLEDGMENTS

My agent, Russ Galen, had been encouraging me for a few years to try my hand at writing a Green Rider novella. I felt like I never had the time to do so because I was always behind on my novels. I did try writing one, but it faltered and I could not resuscitate it. Russ persisted, and then the Berry sisters started talking to me, and *voila! The Dream Gatherer* came into being. It was a satisfying experience to write a 21,500 word story that took mere months to write, as opposed to a 250,000 word behemoth that took *years*. Thanks for pushing me, Russ. Maybe I'll write another one sometime.

DAW Books is known for publishing massive tomes of epic fantasy, so it surprised me when my editor, Betsy Wollheim, wanted to publish *The Dream Gatherer* as a "little book." The novella was, by itself, a little too short for physical book form, so why not add a story? Why not two? And maybe an introduction. And yes, she would let me use my own amateur illustrations for the interior. I confess I kinda got carried away. Or, at least, that's what I thought, because then they requested MORE. How many? As many as I could do—aaaahhhh!! In any case, I am grateful for Betsy's support of my books and the world of the Green Riders over all these years, and I thank her for her willingness to publish this "little book." (And maybe for opening the door to a new career in illustration? Nah. Donato's job is VERY secure.)

Julie Czerneda and I sold our first books to DAW in the same year—1996. However, hers, *A Thousand Words for Stranger,* came out a year before mine. We got to know each other online, then eventually met in person at World Fantasy in Montreal (2001). I became one of her groupies (a happy bunch known as *Czernedians*). She also introduced me to butter tarts! She was not only a friend, but a guide when it came to publishing. I could go to her to get her read on certain situations and ask questions. I admit there are times when she terrifies me, especially when salmon puffs are in the offing, but you won't meet a sharper, savvier, wiser author than Julie. By the way, she writes strong character-based science fiction and fantasy and has numerous titles to her name. If you haven't read her work, I encourage you to look it up. Thank you, Julie, for all the years of friendship and fun, and for graciously creating the introduction to this book.

My thanks to my friend Mel (MelBob) Rice for her feedback on the stories in this book.

Thank you to Donato for painting such a perfect cover for *The Dream Gatherer.*

Here is a re-thank you to Terry Goodkind, who gave of his precious time to me when I was starting out.

Thank you to my support crew over the years, my four-legged companions who have kept me sane on this twenty-year journey. I am not sure this writing life would be worthwhile without them. All but the last two have since passed: Batwing, Percy, Earl Grey, Gryphon, Watson, and Bella. I love you guys always and forever.

To all those Greenies and dreamers out there, happy twentieth and thanks for coming along for the ride. Let's see what adventures the next twenty years bring!

"MISS B"

K. Britain

ABOUT THE AUTHOR

Kristen Britain is the author of the bestselling Green Rider Series. She can be found in the high desert of the American Southwest, hanging with the lizards, napping, and taking orders from the cats. You can visit her website at www.kristenbritain.com